BROKEN ANVILS

The only impossible journey is the one you never begin

ROHITH AGARWAL

INDIA · SINGAPORE · MALAYSIA

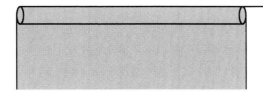

TABLE OF
CONTENTS

Table of Contents

Table of Contents

CHAPTER 1

ARRIVAL

The hissing of gas cutters and the distinctive metallic clang of hammers hitting anvils filled the air as a weary Jeevan made his way through the compound. He looked up to see the enormous mass in front of him. The word *Herald Doña Paz* was carved on the side of the hull and two workers continued to saw their way through the metal body.

Jeevan closed his eyes for a second. He had just gotten off the train earlier that morning. It had been a tiring journey of almost two days from his home back in West Bengal and he hadn't eaten anything for almost that long. It's not like he didn't want to, he didn't have the money. He had walked the entirety of the seven kilometres from the station to the shipbreaking compound in the scorching heat and his legs felt like they would fall off his body. He had already seen quite a few things on his way, things he had never seen before at home. He had seen underground trains, so many cars on the road that he lost count, and the vast expanse of the sea. He even saw a huge banner addressing global warming, an issue he had studied back in his childhood but never paid much attention to.

But even after all this, his tired face glowed, almost as if he had waited his entire life to get an opportunity to look at this ship, this compound. He had heard a great deal about the shipbreaking industry from Ravi *chacha* back at his home in Amjhuri which was a small village within the Bankura district in West Bengal. Ravi *chacha* had said that he worked in the industry and had been asked to recruit young and strong men who could work in the yard. He had heard that the workers were provided good housing facilities with their own colonies to live in, water to use throughout the day and clean sanitary toilets accessible at all times.

All of this sounded like a dream to Jeevan compared to the living conditions at home which included a thatched hut with a roof made of tin and one small room which could hardly accommodate two grown men. In this hut nested a family of five with the kitchen, bedroom, and dining all in one. The one toilet in the entire village that had running water was situated two kilometres away from his home so defecating in the open was something he had become used to. Jeevan opened his eyes again and looked up. The rays of the sun hit his eyes directly forcing him to squint.

He considered himself lucky to have come across Ravi *chacha* as he was later told that *chacha* would leave the very next day to look for suitable people in the next village. As instructed, he looked around trying to spot a man wearing a yellow hat and jacket. After several minutes, he finally spotted an office within which a morbidly obese man sat on a chair. He was sleeping with his legs up on the table, and his face was covered by a yellow hat. He walked up to the office and knocked on the door in an attempt to wake the man, but only got a loud snore in response.

Jeevan could not believe how peacefully the man was sleeping amidst the constant hammering and ear-piercing screeching of the electric saws being used outside. He walked inside the office and saw that it was a small room with a wooden desk placed in the centre. Jeevan covered his nose as a strong stench suddenly invaded the air around him. The room reeked of tobacco and alcohol and he noticed empty beer bottles lying around. He approached the table and cleared his throat loudly, hoping to bring the man out of his otherworldly slumber. A muffled grunting noise escaped the man's throat as he struggled to sit up. He took the cap off and placed it on the table. He looked at Jeevan in a way that made him feel like the man would wring his neck on the spot if he had the chance.

"Kya hua? Kaun hai tu?" asked the man, demanding to know who Jeevan was as he scanned him from head to toe.

Jeevan understood bits and pieces of Hindi as he had spent some time in his childhood with an old woman next door who used to speak the language. The woman had passed away years ago so he never got a chance to develop his knowledge.

He timidly brought out a piece of paper and placed it on the table. The man grabbed the paper and instantly smiled revealing a bright reddish black set of teeth that had lost their original colour due to the heavy and constant use of tobacco and betel leaves.

"*Ek aur aa gaya jungle se,*" grinned the man referring to Jeevan as one more person from the wild.

Jeevan felt his heart sink. Despite his broken understanding of the language, he instantly knew what the man had meant. After all, this was not the first time he had been discriminated against due to his tribal origins.

"I'm your supervisor, Raghuvir. You will be working in the gas cutting section," stated the man. "Go find your tools and get to work."

He pointed towards a wooden shed in front of the office. Jeevan looked at the shed and started making his way towards it when he felt his stomach growl. He remembered that he hadn't eaten anything in the last two days. He looked back at the man and tried to speak but stopped instantly. He wanted to ask for food but didn't know how.

"What happened?" asked the man in a noticeably unkind tone, looking almost angry as he waited for Jeevan to respond.

"*Khawar,*" mumbled Jeevan in his mother tongue.

But the supervisor did not understand Bengali.

"What in God's name are you saying?" he asked, this time in a deeper and more menacing voice.

Jeevan was a little intimidated. He made a signal with his hand pointing towards his mouth, desperately trying to express his hunger.

"You want to eat?" the man asked.

Jeevan's face lit up and he nodded eagerly. Suddenly the man burst out laughing.

"You want to eat? Do you think this is your father's yard that we will give you free meals?"

Jeevan was stunned. He could not believe what he had just heard.

"Now get to work before I come there and hammer some sense into you," said Raghuvir.

Jeevan once again slowly started making his way out of the office, ignoring the constant pangs in his stomach. He knew he had to get out or he would be berated again.

He stepped out of the office and stared at the huge plot of land in front of him. The entire expanse was covered by dismantled bodies of ships. It was a bright sunny day but the air around the yard wore a coat of thick smog. Wherever Jeevan's wandering gaze stopped, he noticed activity. There were people all over the place, on the ship's body, underneath it, some hanging by ropes from the side of the hull. Jeevan noticed a lot of people using a specific tool which appeared to throw out a concentrated stream of fire which they would then use to cut the body of the ship.

Jeevan found this very fascinating and figured that this might be the gas cutting process that the supervisor Raghuvir had told him about. One thing Jeevan noticed was the huge amount of smoke being released due to this gas cutting, which was constantly feeding the smog coat making it ever thicker. He made his way to the shed where he found the tools that looked similar to the ones being used out there. He picked them up and went towards the first ship he had seen when he came in.

He saw about five to six men sitting on the hull of the ship, chipping away chunks of the metal with their gas cutters. Jeevan approached one of them and tried to ask him what to do but the man looked back at him with a completely blank expression not understanding a word he had just said. Jeevan was suddenly overtaken by an intense feeling of shame and inferiority. He walked away, mumbling something to himself.

"I will learn more Hindi and will converse with these people soon, just wait," said Jeevan to himself in a tone that he had hoped to be reassuring but felt dejected.

He found a corner where he placed his tools and belongings and started looking around for help. He observed the other workers operate the gas cutter and being the quick learner that he had been from a tender age, Jeevan quickly figured out how to get the tool going. He directed it towards the iron and was just about to make contact when he heard a sudden commotion behind him.

Raghuvir had come up to the ship in the meantime and had started an argument with one of the workers.

"Just 5 pieces!" shouted Raghuvir.

The worker, an old man in his late fifties was kneeling in front of Raghuvir with folded hands. He had an extremely tired and apologetic look on his face.

"This is the third time this week," continued the supervisor. "I won't take this anymore, you're leaving today."

"Please *sahib,* give me another chance," the old man pleaded. He had tears in his eyes and his voice was quivering, clearly intimidated as he spoke. "I have six children to feed. My elder son and I are the only ones who support our family and we haven't even gotten our wages for the last 3 days. If you make me go, we'll be destroyed, *sahib.*"

He suddenly fell at Raghuvir's feet and burst out crying. Raghuvir pulled his feet away from the man's hand knocking the helmet off his head in the process.

"Don't you dare touch me, you peasant," he spat out.

Jeevan was shocked by the entire incident that unfolded in front of him. He didn't know how to react. He stared at the old man and a fleeting image of his old and sick father back home crossed his mind. He suddenly felt his hands tighten into a fist, his heartbeat getting faster and faster as he looked at Raghuvir.

"*Baba,*" came a loud voice from amongst the crowd that had now gathered around the two.

Jeevan kept watching as a boy pushed his way out of the crowd. He had a very young face but the daily rigorous activity of moving shipbreaking materials had developed his body into that of a grown man. He bolted towards his father.

"Are you okay, *baba*?" asked the boy, his face scrunched up with worry.

Raghuvir glared at them and said, "Get out of here right now."

The boy slowly helped his father get up and started checking him thoroughly, looking for injuries on his body. The old man, still crying inconsolably, embraced his son. Then suddenly Jeevan noticed the air around the young boy change. The worried look on his face was wiped off in an instant and was replaced by a look which Jeevan perceived as being full of malice and hatred.

"You shouldn't have done this," growled the boy through tightened lips.

Raghuvir was clearly taken aback at this sudden resistance.

"What did you say?" he asked, his voice significantly lower than what it was just a few moments ago.

"You knew he was ill and suffering. The whole yard knows," the boy said in a calm but dead voice. "You still made him work extra hard. You did not pay him for days on end after making him work."

"He asked me to keep quiet despite all this," he continued, looking down at his father. "But not this time, just wait and watch," were his last words before he started walking out of the yard with his father leaning on him.

The supervisor stared at them as they walked away. He made a gurgling noise with his mouth and dropped a big fat red globule of tobacco-stained saliva on the ground. He then adjusted his pants which could barely contain his immense belly and walked towards the centre of the yard where he picked a bell and rang it. It resounded with a screech throughout the yard.

"Today's work is over. Head back home now and collect your wages later tomorrow," shouted Raghuvir looking around the yard. His voice was a little louder and sterner while he provided the latter information.

Jeevan could hear a collective sigh from around him as the supervisor made this announcement.

"Again," Jeevan heard someone muttering behind him.

"How am I supposed to feed my family like this?" another voice chimed in.

Jeevan turned around to see a group of middle-aged men huddled together and packing their things while talking amongst themselves. For a moment he thought he would approach them but anxiety got the better of him. The men stood up and started walking towards the entrance of the yard. It struck Jeevan that they may be returning to the labour colonies made by the government for the yard workers. Once again, he had gotten this information from Ravi *chacha*. Jeevan's face lit up. He thought he would finally get some food and a place to sleep after two long nights of sleeplessness. He quickly picked up the sack of clothes which he had carried all the way from West Bengal and started following the group of men, trying to stay unnoticed all the while. Jeevan figured that it would be better to get things done by himself than to ask the supervisor for help and get scolded.

CHAPTER 2

DADA

The weather was pleasant. There was a gentle yet cool breeze flowing through the area, dragging a solitary leaf through the road as a car passed by, suddenly disturbing the tranquillity of the sun-kissed evening. The car halted at a red traffic light as a group of men with hammers and pickaxes on their shoulders crossed the road in front of it, followed by another man a few seconds later.

As Jeevan crossed the road, he looked at the car and saw a family of four sitting inside. There were two kids in the back with a dog and the parents sat in front. Jeevan saw happiness in front of him. He could see the kids laughing and the parents talking to each other with big smiles on their faces. Suddenly the woman looked at Jeevan, the two pairs of eyes making contact. She whispered something to her husband and the man turned around to look at Jeevan staring at them. He lowered the window of the car and beckoned him.

Jeevan was taken aback. He wondered why rich people like them would want to talk to somebody like him, an outsider. He slowly made his way to the vehicle and the man stuck his hand out. He held a fifty rupee note between his index and middle finger. Jeevan didn't know how to respond. These people were offering him money. He took it and looked at it like someone had stolen the most precious diamond in the world and given it to him. The man rolled his window up and sped away, the car's engine making a loud revving noise as Jeevan watched it disappear around the corner. He neatly folded the money twice and put it in a small pouch that he brought out from his pants. With a smile on his face, he started following his fellow workers.

It had been around twenty minutes since they had left the yard. They had entered the main city area by now. Jeevan, though tired and exhausted, turned his head from left to right and then from top to bottom, clearly excited to see the brick houses and skyscrapers around him. The commotion in the main city was unlike anything he had experienced. He had managed to remain completely ignorant of the urban lifestyle as he had grown and spent the first twenty-five years of his life in a remote village. One thing that had been bothering Jeevan for a while but something that he had decided not to give much thought to was the fact that they had been walking for so long. He remembered Ravi *chacha* saying that the colonies were fairly close to the working grounds to make the commute convenient for the workers.

Jeevan had just started getting second thoughts about his decision to follow the workers when they suddenly took a sharp turn down an extremely narrow alleyway between two big buildings. The entrance was barely big enough to let one grown man go through at a time. By the time Jeevan reached it, all the men had passed through it, one by one. Jeevan placed the sack with his belongings on his head and passed through the entrance of the alley.

He made a slight retching noise as a strong odour hit his nose. He looked in front of him to see a narrow stretch of wet and slimy road, a long drain running along the side, the contents of which were an ungodly mixture of yellow and green. He covered his nose and slowly made his way through the alley, treading lightly, trying to avoid slipping on the slimy texture and falling.

He walked through the alley for a good couple of minutes before it finally gave way to a bigger area. Jeevan exited the alley into a lot of commotion. At first, he thought that there was some sort of an argument going on. Jeevan started looking around for his fellow workers. The area was big and had a water body surrounding it. There was a stench coming from the water body which made Jeevan realize that it was the sewage disposal system of the entire city. The plot was lined with numerous thatched tin huts, which had people inside, some cooking, some sleeping, and some washing clothes outside their huts. Jeevan still hadn't been able to find any known faces and suddenly felt a feeling of fear wash over him. He didn't know what to do, didn't know anyone, and didn't know how to speak the native language. He felt very lost. Suddenly he heard the commotion behind him break up as a man wearing a checkered shirt and black pants with neatly combed hair walked out of the gathering.

"Positively pay your rent by the end of this week, *mausi,*" he said with an accent that felt strikingly familiar to Jeevan.

The man turned around and started walking towards the alley when he noticed Jeevan staring at him. The man had a confused look on his face at first but his expression changed in a moment almost as if he recognised Jeevan.

"Are you the new worker who was supposed to arrive from West Bengal today?" he asked Jeevan and was met with an earnest nod in response.

"Do you speak Bengali?" asked the man in Jeevan's mother tongue.

Jeevan's expression changed. He had finally found someone he could ask questions to, someone who would explain what in God's name was going on and someone who could finally help him get some food.

"Yes, *dada,*" croaked Jeevan, his voice hoarse from his clearly parched throat.

The man couldn't help but smile upon noticing the sudden relief on an otherwise aggravated face. He walked up to Jeevan and looked at him from top to bottom.

Jeevan was wearing a tattered white *baniyan* which revealed his lean yet muscular stature. It was covered with dust and dirt from his long day at the yard and so were the short blue cargo pants which had a hole on the left side. The man noticed two big scars on Jeevan's left arm, which could be easily missed due to his otherwise dark complexion.

"What is your name?" asked the man in a kind voice, continuing to speak in Bengali.

"Jeevan, *dada.*"

"Your hut is down that lane to the left," said the man pointing behind Jeevan.

Jeevan looked confused. He had so many questions but didn't know which one to ask first.

"Can I get some food, *dada?*" asked Jeevan very timidly.

"You haven't eaten anything in the entire day?" the man asked with a surprised look on his face.

Jeevan shook his head. The man asked him to wait for a few moments before returning to the gathering. He said something inaudible to them.

A few minutes later, he returned to Jeevan and said, "Come with me."

CHAPTER 3

REASSURANCE

The small rubber tip shook vigorously making a rattling noise before giving way to an intense burst of hot air, making a loud hissing noise in the process. An old woman, probably in her late sixties, picked it up from the stove and placed it on the ground. It was around seven in the evening, almost over an hour after the sun had set but the city of Bhavnagar was still as busy as ever.

"Give him another *paratha, chachi,*" said the man, burping loudly in the process.

The food stall, though small, was surrounded by eight or nine people waiting for their food and another ten or fifteen sitting and eating the food they had ordered. Within the stall, an old woman and a boy who looked like her son were working nonstop in order to keep up with the number of orders coming in.

Jeevan had been staring at the two of them for a while when the man, who had introduced himself as Satya ordered another *paratha,* pulling him out of the trance.

"No *dada,* let it be, I'm full," smiled Jeevan, with a feeling of contentment after two long days.

"Then just get me a *chai* and the bill," he yelled again.

"So, what are you going to do now?" asked Satya, looking at Jeevan.

The two of them had been talking for a while now and Jeevan had told him everything—how he had come to know about this work, the things he had been promised, and the things that had happened earlier that day.

At that time Satya let him know that his Ravi *chacha* had lied to him about a lot of things. Firstly, there were no housing colonies for the labourers left. The government had assigned seven colonies out of which only two were usable and they had been permanently occupied by workers for quite some time now.

Jeevan half listened and wondered while looking at the boy and his mother working in the stall. His thoughts took him to their own thatched hut at home where he imagined his old mother sitting beside the small mud stove, cooking and coughing now and then like she had been for quite some time now. Jeevan wanted to go home. His insides were screaming for him to go back home but he knew he couldn't.

When he left, he had not been on good terms with his family. His mother had pleaded with him to not go away to some far-off city where she wouldn't be able to see him. Others had warned him against Ravi *chacha*. But Jeevan hadn't paid attention to any of these people.

He had gathered whatever money he could, packed his clothes and left. He had barely enough for buying a train ticket. He had promised himself that he would send money home the moment he started earning so that they wouldn't have to sleep on an empty stomach again. But now he had no money and was homeless in the middle of an unknown city. Satya, almost as if invading Jeevan's mind and reading his thoughts, looked at him and put a hand on his shoulder.

"You can work here, my friend," he said. Jeevan seemed unsure about what Satya had just said.

"Do you know how important the daily work that you're going to do here is?" asked Satya.

The young boy from the stall approached the table and placed a tray containing a steaming cup of tea and a piece of paper on it. Satya picked both up, took a sip from the cup and continued to explain how the ship metal, especially steel that they break, is recycled and used to make several new products. This lowers the demand for mined iron ore and reduces energy use in the steel-making industry, ultimately helping the economy. Satya also explained how the industry employs tens of thousands of other helpless people like Jeevan, giving them a chance to earn and feed their families.

"I know it's not ideal and not what you expected it to be but you can work and earn enough money to make something out of yourself, Jeevan."

Jeevan turned his head and looked at Satya, his eyes glistening and a solitary tear flowed down his cheek before he asked, "Do you really think so?"

"I know so," came a warm reassuring smile from the other man.

CHAPTER 4

A NEW BEGINNING

It was well past eight at night when Satya and Jeevan returned to the slum. To Jeevan, it felt like he had travelled from one world to another in a matter of a few minutes—from the busy bustle of the streets of Bhavnagar to this slum which had a deathly silence surrounding it. There was a certain impending gloom in the air which felt like the 'calm before the storm.'

Jeevan felt slightly unsettled as they walked through the area towards his hut. It was now his home, thought Jeevan to himself.

They came to a halt as Satya paused and pointed towards a cluster of small tin huts and said, "The one in the middle is yours."

Jeevan looked at it for a while before slowly approaching the doorway, stopping just in front of it.

He turned back towards Satya and asked, "When will I see you again, *dada*?"

Satya looked at Jeevan, knowing that he wouldn't like the answer. "I visit once every month to collect the rent from everyone here," he said.

Jeevan's face dropped as Satya started walking back towards the entrance of the slum.

"The next time I see you, you'll owe me two hundred and fifty rupees," he said loudly and smiled one last time before turning round the corner and disappearing from Jeevan's sight.

Jeevan smiled slightly and turned to enter his new home. The room was unbelievably small. It had one small cot, a small kitchen which could barely fit a small man and a brick wall in the middle separating the kitchen from the sleeping area. Jeevan looked around but already knew that there was no space for a bathroom inside. He put down his sack of clothes and opened it, taking a small picture out. It was a picture of a young girl with bright eyes and very sharp features. Jeevan brushed two fingers over the picture and then touched his lips with the finger.

"Goodnight, love," he smiled, looking at the picture before placing it back in the sack and lying down on the cot.

Then he started practising Hindi words verbally, something he had been doing for a few days now, in preparation for a new beginning. Several minutes later, he put his hand over his eyes and closed them, the tiredness completely engulfing him as he fell asleep almost instantly.

CHAPTER 5

NIGHTMARE

The smell of rain filled the area as a cool breeze replaced the previously humid air, a humidity Jeevan was far too familiar with. He looked around to see the same greenery, the same flowing river and the same banyan tree that he had seen during his entire childhood. He was back home in West Bengal. He looked up to see the hulking growth of a tree above him, a cluster of other small branches stemming from the original tree making it almost impossible to determine which one was the actual trunk.

But Jeevan knew it well. The banyan tree in front of him was more than a hundred years old, or so the villagers and his parents believed. He navigated his way amongst the growth almost like he had daily practice and quickly reached the thick trunk in the middle of the cluster. There he walked around the circumference of the tree until his eyes fell on something and stopped. He touched the wood with his hands, running them over the writing etched on the trunk.

"Jeevan loves Bhoomi."

Jeevan smiled sheepishly as he ran his fingers over her name.

"Jeevan!" came a voice reverberating through foliage. Jeevan turned around almost instantly hearing the all too familiar voice.

"Jeevan, are you there?" the voice came again.

"Bhoomi, I'm here," he replied as he made his way out of the growth just as easily as he had made his way in.

He raced out to see his childhood love, his best friend, and his constant companion ever since he was a baby. She was standing there in front of the banyan tree, slightly wet from the drizzle outside, and now she stood in front of him. She was wet but Jeevan could make out the tears in her eyes as she dropped down to her knees and started crying. He ran towards her and held her shoulders in an attempt to comfort her.

"Don't worry, Bhoomi. I have a proper job now, I earn money. Now your father can't say no to our marriage," he said in a reassuring tone.

"You were too late, Jeevan," she said, looking into his eyes. "My father married me off two days after you left. He said you would never come back here."

Jeevan let go of her and sat down on the wet ground beside her, his mouth slightly ajar. He could not believe what he was hearing. He stared at the sky which was now turning even darker than before. The silence in the air was accompanied by a deathly chill. A good couple of minutes had passed before Jeevan mustered the strength to speak again.

"How are you doing? How is he?" he asked, trying to enquire about the groom.

"They treat me well and with respect. I am happy there, Jeevan," she replied, her eyes locked on the tree line in the distance.

Jeevan stretched out his hand and placed his palm on hers, squeezing it gently and said in a low voice, "Come with me. I'm earning money now. Together we'll be happy in a new place away from all these people who want to control us. Come with me and..."

Jeevan could not finish what he was saying as Bhoomi yanked her hand out of his grip and yelled, "I can't be so selfish. You left me! You left your family and now you're asking me to do the same. Your mother is dead because of you."

Bhoomi got up and started walking in the opposite direction as Jeevan stared at her, unable to say anything, a feeling of guilt gripping his heart tightly.

"Your mother is dead because of you," came the voice echoing through his thoughts again. His eyes widened. He hadn't comprehended it earlier.

"What did she say?" Jeevan asked himself, his heart now picking up pace.

He got up and started sprinting towards his village as the downpour got stronger. It took him over ten minutes to reach his home by the end of which he was panting and coughing. But his fear kept him going. At last, he finally caught a glimpse of the thatched hut, its state as sorry as ever, sitting on the dead plot of land that his family had tried to sow on multiple occasions. But every time, the crop was a failure. He made his way to the entrance and heard wails from inside. He could hear his father's voice too.

He walked in to see his mother, covered up to the neck with a white sheet, her skin pale as snow. His other family members including his brother and father sat around her, the three of them forming a circle, howling with tears in their eyes.

Jeevan was feeling overwhelmed, he did not know how to react. It had been six years since his father's demise now, following which his family's condition had rapidly deteriorated. Seeing his father, alive, sitting and crying beside his now-dead mother, he felt as if he would lose his mind.

"This is all because of you," a voice came from somewhere amidst the crowd.

Jeevan looked up to see his father staring at him, eyes red and bright as he repeated, "It's all your fault. You left them alone. You took all the money."

The voice grew louder as Jeevan suddenly woke up, hyperventilating, his face drenched in sweat. He reached for the jug of water beside his bed and gulped down all of it in an instant. It took him a while to process the nightmare. Several minutes later Jeevan lay back down and stared outside the small window as the first rays of the morning sun lit the sky giving it a light blue hue. A feeling of loneliness engulfed Jeevan as he turned around and closed his eyes to get some sleep.

CHAPTER 6

MAKING A FRIEND

The sun was scorching, making the steel wreckage around the yard radiate heat. Jeevan was wearing a white hat, the insides of which were drenched from the excessive perspiration in this unbearably hot weather. It had been about a couple of hours since Jeevan had arrived at the yard, the majority of which he had spent trying to figure out the gas cutting machinery. He had faced numerous problems in the meantime but didn't lose his patience. With every problem he faced, he took his time to look around and observe the other people using the gas cutters.

Once again, he guided the nozzle of the gas cutter towards the steel and started the apparatus. The concentrated burst of fire hit the steel and made a hole right through it in a matter of seconds. The machine offered a certain recoil when switched on, something he had not gotten used to yet, making it difficult for him to maintain a straight line while cutting the sheets. This resulted in uneven shapes every time he cut a piece of metal off. Slowly but surely, Jeevan got the hang of the entire process and it wasn't long before he, like everyone else, had started cutting perfect rectangular sheets of steel which were then carried by the loaders and placed in big trucks. He had already seen about three of these trucks leave the yard, none of which had come back yet.

A bead of sweat ran down Jeevan's nose and fell on the hot metal in front of him, making a slight sizzling noise as he finished cutting yet another piece of metal. He looked to his left to see the pile of sheets that had now accumulated by his side. He was reminded of the things Satya had told him the night before, at the food stall. All the metal he was cutting would be used to make something new, something useful that would help another human being in some way. Jeevan felt proud of himself. He was finally doing something useful.

"I wish mother could see me now," Jeevan whispered to himself, a fleeting memory of the nightmare crossing his mind momentarily.

He placed the sheet on top of the others and took his helmet off. His face was completely drenched in sweat and his hair was matted over his forehead. He used his hands to wipe the sweat off and placed the helmet on the ground. The gas cutting had given rise to a thick layer of smoke which was now surrounding the entire area of the wreckage. Jeevan took a deep breath in, feeling the muscles in his arms throb and his fingers ache. He suddenly felt a weird irritation in his throat and started coughing vigorously.

There were four other workers with Jeevan who were assigned to disassembling that particular ship that day. All of them snapped their heads and looked at Jeevan in unison.

"He needs water," one of them said before another man got up and ran towards Jeevan, grabbing him and guiding him towards a clearing, away from all the cutting and hissing.

"Wait here," said the man to Jeevan before walking away from him and disappearing around the corner.

Jeevan had been coughing all this while, his eyes red and watery by now. His suffering went on for the next two or three minutes which seemed like an eternity to him before the man returned with a big jug full of water and offered it to him. He took the jug and splashed it on his face before lifting the jug over his head and tilting it making the water fall directly into his mouth. He gulped down greedily, almost instantly feeling considerably better.

The man looked at him and smiled, saying, "It's the smoke. It takes some time to get used to."

Jeevan seemed confused. "It's okay," the man laughed aloud. "This has happened to all of us at some point while working here."

Jeevan politely handed the jug of water back to the man and bent his head in an attempt to express his gratitude.

"That goes to the other side of the yard," said the man pointing towards the jug in Jeevan's hand. "Come, I'll show you where," he added and started walking.

Jeevan quickly caught up with him and walked beside him as they crossed the yard to reach the other end where there was a water pipe beside the supervisor's office. Jeevan was asked to place the jug beside the water pipe. The two men then started making their way back towards their side of the yard.

"I'm guessing you don't speak much Hindi?" asked the man about halfway through.

Jeevan shook his head. Disheartenment was written clearly on his face.

"Don't worry," smiled the man once again. "As long as you understand us."

Jeevan's face lit up at this unexpectedly friendly gesture. For the first time in a while, he felt comfortable. It was reassuring for him to know that he could rely on the people at work.

"*Dhanyavaad, dada,*" a low, but quiet whisper escaped his lips.

"Not *dada*, Aman. That's my name," the man replied.

The duo had almost made their way back to the wreckage when something caught Jeevan's attention and he slowed down. Aman followed his gaze, rolling his eyes and letting out a sigh as if instantly reading Jeevan's mind.

Jeevan had spotted another water tap, this one immediately next to the area where they were working. He wondered why they had to cross the entire yard to get some water when it was available right here.

He looked at Aman in an attempt to give his thoughts some voice but before he got a chance, Aman started speaking, "That one doesn't work. When it does, it's all gunk and dirt."

Jeevan stared at him incredulously, clearly dissatisfied with this situation.

"There is one other tap that doesn't work. The one beside Raghuvir's office is the only one that does," Aman continued. "It is the same for bathrooms. There are just two, one of which you can use. The other one is locked and only Raghuvir has the key. Since there are so many workers and only one working toilet, we prefer going out in the open."

When Aman finished speaking, he looked at Jeevan and gave him a playful wink. He then walked up to his spot, put on his helmet and started cutting away at the metal again followed by a clearly distracted Jeevan.

CHAPTER 7

THE RICH AND THE POOR

The late evening sun glowed warmly as Jeevan made his way back to the slum. The day had passed in a blur and he had spent most of it thinking about the things his co-worker Aman had said to him.

It was unfair that the workers did not get the necessary facilities in the compound. Jeevan had only spent a couple of days here now but he knew exactly how exhausting the work could be. He knew that they were entitled to the water and toilet facilities as Satya had told him that though it was the government who provided these facilities, there were some corrupt individuals like their own supervisor who did not keep up with the maintenance so that they could earn some extra money.

"Some extra money at the cost of others' misery," Jeevan thought to himself as he walked down the busy street.

He instinctively reached around and smiled with satisfaction as he felt the rattling of coins within the pouch tied around his waist. Jeevan had gotten his wage today and he was beside himself. It was his first salary, money he had earned himself. He had worked hard for it and it was not ideal but he was proud of himself. He wished to have his family around to see him. He could tell all of them that they were wrong.

A loud commotion snapped Jeevan back to reality as he entered a busy market with people walking around as far as the eye could see. There were a variety of shops selling vegetables, meat and other groceries that caught Jeevan's attention. The realisation dawned on him again that he was living completely alone in a new city. This time the feeling struck him with greater intensity.

He started making a mental list of all the things he would need for his home. Food was the first thing that crossed his mind along with a slight rumbling in his belly. He looked around and his gaze fell upon a shop selling meat. Meat was a rarity back home. In fact, Jeevan could almost mentally count the number of times he had eaten chicken in his entire life. He slowly made his way over to the shop and took his pouch out, untying its thread. Suddenly he felt a push from behind as a man dressed all in white crossed him and stood in front of him.

"Chotu, three kilograms for me. Fast," said the man in an incredibly impolite voice.

He then made a gurgling sound and spat on the ground right in front of Jeevan. But Jeevan was too distracted to notice any of this. He had his eyes fixed on the man cutting the chicken pieces one by one. He then gathered up all the pieces and weighed them. Jeevan had made up his mind about having chicken for dinner. He approached the shopkeeper timidly and put up one finger, trying to ask for a kilo of chicken.

"*Ek* kilo?" the shopkeeper confirmed before getting to work and giving Jeevan a black plastic bag full of meat a few seconds later.

Jeevan took the bag with a childish smile on his face as he opened his pouch and waited to pay the man.

"*Teen,*" said the man, putting up three fingers.

"Three hundred?!" Jeevan couldn't believe what he was hearing.

For a moment he thought the man was being dishonest but then he remembered how much money the man before him had paid. He had not considered the price of the meat in his excited state. Jeevan's daily wage was three hundred and fifty rupees only, which he had thought to be a significant amount because he never really had a chance to deal with money during his entire teenage years, given his family's condition.

He sheepishly placed the plastic bag back on the counter and took off at a half-trotting pace and almost instantly disappeared amidst the crowd. By the time he got back, the sun had set and darkness had completely engulfed the entire slum area due to the lack of any light sources.

Jeevan had his arms wrapped around two big bags as he entered his shack. He put the bags down and took the vegetables and other things that he bought earlier at the market out.

He then took the small pouch out again and counted the money remaining inside. It was exactly one hundred and forty-two rupees. He took a moment to look at the things he had bought with just over two hundred rupees and couldn't help but compare the price of that small portion of meat earlier, to all this. It seemed almost comical to him how the man in white at the meat shop had bought three kilograms without giving it any thought. He tried to do the math as to how much three kilograms of chicken would cost but failed. Being able to spend money like that was a dream for him. Jeevan smiled sadly and started making arrangements for his meal.

CHAPTER 8

STEEL HEARTS

It had been a month since Jeevan had arrived in Gujarat. These thirty days had proved to be pretty uneventful with him repeating the same routine every day, morning to evening. The workers were supposed to report to the yard by eight in the morning and were allowed to leave after five in the evening, after a full day's work. The day's toil would leave Jeevan devoid of the will and energy to go exploring in the city afterwards. He used to go out once a week to get the required groceries and supplies, but that was pretty much the extent of it.

Some things had changed though. He had gotten considerably better at speaking Hindi, thanks to his daily practice. Aman, his co-worker also had a part to play in this development. He would converse with Jeevan at length and would point out the mistakes he made.

The day had started like any other, except today Jeevan was missing a particular person back home. He sat really close to the body of the ship and guided the torch in his hand very carefully as he carved a small heart out of the metal. The shape of the steel heart seemed a bit off, so Jeevan repeated the process. Before he knew it he had a small pile of hearts lying in front of him, more than he could count. He was thinking about Bhoomi but he knew that a part of his nightmare had been fuelled by actual events in his life. Jeevan had made no promises to Bhoomi before leaving despite knowing the fact that her father had made plans to marry her off.

They had been hiding their love for each other for quite some time now and Bhoomi had already turned down four potential matches, hoping that Jeevan would be the one for her. But the pressure was increasing and they knew that her father would force the fifth marriage on her. But he had still chosen to leave. His fascination for a new life in a new city was given priority over his childhood love as he left promising to return for her. But he knew that it was already too late, he just did not dare to face reality.

Jeevan picked one small but perfectly shaped heart up from the pile. He stared at it as he remembered his love, unmindful of the fact that he had left the gas for the torch on. After a few seconds, he picked up the torch and started working again. The overflowing gas suddenly gave way to a burst of flame, considerably bigger than usual, taking Jeevan by surprise. He instantly turned it off, but not before the flame made contact with one of his fingers directly, making him squeal in pain.

After a few seconds, his finger started to change colour. Jeevan got up and crossed over to the other side of the yard hastily where he washed his finger with cold water. It felt a little better but the pain was still quite unbearable.

He held his finger as he walked back to his spot slowly, not knowing what to do next. Upon reaching his spot, Jeevan was greeted by a new face. A woman, older than him, stood there with a white box in her hand, patiently waiting for him.

"Let me see your hand," she said in a soft but raspy voice, the smoke making her cough slightly as she took his hand and inspected it.

She then took an ointment from the box and applied it to his finger before finally wrapping it with a clean white gauze pad. All this while, Jeevan stared at the woman, her face reminding him of the girl back home.

"Dhanyavaad," he said sheepishly after the woman finished patching him up.

She stared and replied with a weak smile before getting up and walking away. Jeevan could not find the strength to break his gaze even as the woman walked away. He kept staring until she disappeared amidst the wreckage.

"Who was the woman? Was she new here? When did she start working?" Questions like these started flooding Jeevan's mind.

He was so engrossed in his thoughts that it took him quite some time to grasp the situation behind him which had heated up. His chain of thoughts was interrupted by the abrupt sound of breaking glass followed by loud screaming as he heard someone crying out for help. He quickly followed the noise and noticed a crowd outside the supervisor's office.

"Where is he?"

"Bring him here. I will kill him today."

Jeevan could not make out a lot from the commotion. Then he suddenly noticed a face which seemed familiar in the crowd. It was the young boy from the day of Jeevan's arrival whom Raghuvir had kicked out of the yard along with his old father. Behind him, he heard people talking amongst themselves.

"His father had come yesterday to collect the pending wages. Raghuvir did not even let him inside the office."

The mob was getting impatient now. Jeevan had just noticed the weapons they were carrying with them. A few of them had wooden bats and sticks but many were carrying long knives with them. Taking a closer look, he realised that every single person in that crowd was drunk. They could barely stand straight, they either screamed or slurred their speech when they opened their mouths.

He quickly realised that these people would actually kill Raghuvir if they caught hold of him. Such was their intent. The only thing stopping them was Raghuvir's absence from work that day, which proved life-saving. All the workers in the yard had ceased their activities and were now staring at the scene, fear written clearly on their faces.

Suddenly a loud shriek was heard as one of the gang members grabbed a worker by his collar, placed a gun near his head and screamed, "Where is he?"

Terror gripped the heart of every individual present there as a deathly silence enveloped the area, a feeling of impending disaster in the air.

It was the young boy who walked up to the man and touched his elbow saying, "Not them."

The words had an effect similar to a hot knife cutting through butter, as he instantly let the worker go and put the gun away.

"Tell him that we were here. Tell him that we will come back for him," the boy shouted loudly before taking off, followed by the mob.

Jeevan watched the entire gang leave as a woman sped past him, crying out as she dropped down beside the worker who had just been held at gunpoint and started asking him repeatedly, "*Aap thik ho, ji?*"

CHAPTER 9

SIGNIFICANT OTHER

"Who, Darpana?" Aman asked Jeevan as the two of them carried a pile of metal sheets over to the loading truck.

It had been a few hours since the gang left and everyone was clearly agitated but Jeevan's fascination with the woman from earlier that day had not ended. He had gone as far as asking Aman about her.

"She has been working here for some time now. Her husband also used to work here. She joined after his death," Aman continued as they dumped the pile on the rest of the wreckage and turned around to get some more.

"Death?" Jeevan's eyes widened. "How did it happen?"

"Shipbreaking claimed him, my friend," Aman replied, a hint of sadness in his voice. "He was working on top of one of the big ships when his equipment failed and he fell from a height of about fifty meters."

Jeevan's eyes widened, the realisation of the constant danger surrounding him in this line of work suddenly hitting him like a train. He always knew that he had to be careful so that he didn't hurt himself while operating the machinery but the risk of losing his life had never once crossed his mind.

"We tried to save him. We rushed him to the facility nearby but it did not have enough to help the poor man. I saw him bleed to death," Aman's voice had completely changed by the time he finished speaking. "Why not take him to a better hospital?" Jeevan asked in a broken but understandable accent.

"It's not so easy, my friend. The good hospitals are quite far away from here. In addition to the distance, they are also very expensive. We have healthcare facilities provided to us by the government nearby but none of them has the equipment or skilled staff to handle an emergency or a major injury," Aman replied without a pause.

Jeevan stopped in his tracks for a few seconds. He couldn't imagine what life must have been for Darpana ever since the incident. The last month hadn't been the easiest for him. He barely had anyone to talk to and the one friend he had, he hadn't been able to meet ever since his first day. He knew what it felt like to be alone and that made him feel weirdly connected to her. He also experienced a strange obligation to try and help the woman in any way he could.

"Where does she work?" asked Jeevan, looking at his co-worker.

A few minutes later, as guided by Aman, Jeevan made his way to the extreme end of the yard where the wreckage ended and the sea began, just beyond the compound. In thirty days, he had been to this area only once because he was never really needed here. Aman had told him that Darpana did not have a fixed working schedule or wage. She was a diversified worker who was sent to work wherever manpower was required.

Jeevan looked for the red and white cabin where she was supposed to working today, noticing it almost instantly at the very end. He walked up to the open door and saw her sitting behind a table, staring out of the window, gaze locked on the horizon. The strong sea breeze played with her long flowing hair as the strands danced around in the air, captivating her spectator's eyes. There was a sudden noise as the breeze made the door slam against the frame, making her look towards it.

She turned around to see Jeevan, his mouth slightly open, and jaw hanging in the air. He looked down the moment they made eye contact. She also noticed the finger wrapped in white and recognised him as the man with the burnt finger, whom she had helped earlier that day.

Darpana approached the doorway and asked, curiosity clear in her eyes, "Can I help you?"

Jeevan tried to reply but could not speak initially. After a few seconds of mumbling and stuttering, he said in broken Hindi, "I wanted to thank you again for helping me."

Darpana giggled at Jeevan's attempt to speak the language and asked him, "How does it feel now? I would give you something for the pain but the medical supply for this month hasn't arrived yet."

Jeevan felt his cheeks turn red as he made another failed attempt at trying to explain how she had already helped him enough.

"Would you like to have some tea?" she asked, taking Jeevan by surprise again. "Actually, I am in charge of canteen duty as well today so I have access to kitchen facilities here."

Jeevan was delighted by this gesture and nodded happily, making her giggle once more. He was asked to sit as she went inside the kitchen and started boiling some water. Jeevan felt his gaze involuntarily lock on her again as she worked in the kitchen.

After nearly five minutes, Darpana noticed him staring and broke the silence by asking, "So what is your name? Where are you from?"

Jeevan's eyes widened, blood rushing to his cheeks. He blushed furiously, realising that she had caught him staring.

"Jeevan. My home is in West Bengal. You?" he asked in return.

Darpana looked out through the window for a brief second, sighed softly as if remembering something and said, "Bihar."

Over the next forty-five minutes, the duo exchanged stories, some emotional and some humorous. For the first time in a while, Jeevan felt like he wasn't alone in the entire world. He felt comfortable enough to let her in on his personal life and told her about everything that had happened back home, till he reached Gujarat.

Jeevan even told her about the immense guilt he was fighting for the condition in which he had left his family and Bhoomi and the nightmares that haunted him from time to time. Darpana sat and listened patiently, looking at him with empathy in her eyes. Her calm aura gave Jeevan the strength and assurance to keep going even through his stuttering and broken Hindi.

After he finished speaking the two of them sat quietly, looking at the ground and she said, "I know what it is like to feel alone."

The compound bell rang loudly, signalling the end of their duties. Jeevan looked at her as she got up, trying to think of a way to prolong the conversation.

"Would you like to walk back home with me? I mean which way are you going?" he asked with a slight stutter in his voice, trying not to sound too imposing.

"I have some work here, you can go back home," Darpana replied.

He instantly detected her reluctance and thanked her once more for her help before getting up to leave.

Darpana paused and then called out to him, "Let's talk again tomorrow."

The yard was supposed to be closed the following day so it was a holiday for the workers.

"*Kal, chutti?*" he asked about the holiday tomorrow.

"Oh yes. Then the day after," Darpana couldn't help giggling again.

Jeevan smiled and nodded, clearly delighted and walked out of the cabin.

CHAPTER 10

PAST SCARS

"Two hundred and fifty, good," Satya smiled as he counted the money Jeevan had given him.

It had been exactly one month and three days since the two of them had seen each other. Satya had come to the slum earlier in the day to collect the rent from everybody after which the two friends had decided to have some tea at the same food stall from the first day.

It had been four days since the incident in the yard with the gang and every day since had been filled with fear and anxiety of a sudden abrupt or violent event. But Jeevan was visibly happy today. He knew they had a lot of catching up to do so he did not delay in telling Satya about the things that had happened over the last few days.

Several minutes later, after patiently listening to him, Satya spoke up, "I'm happy to see that you've made so much progress in such little time."

Jeevan looked at him, his eyes glowing like that of a nine-year-old. On several occasions when circumstances hadn't favoured him, he had kept reassuring himself that he was doing well and would figure a way out. But somehow, getting that same encouragement from someone else gave him immense joy.

"*Dada,* your bill," said the young boy manning the food stall, suddenly interrupting the conversation.

Satya picked up the piece of paper and took his wallet out when he noticed Jeevan slide a ten rupee note on the table and say, "This is for my share. Thank you for paying the last time."

Satya's face lit up as he stared back with admiration and respect. It had been a couple of hours since nightfall and the two were making their way back home. Satya had noticed Jeevan's distraction for some time now.

He was about to express the same when Jeevan spoke up, "How does one become a supervisor?"

Satya showed a glint of curiosity and asked, "May I ask why are you asking a question like that suddenly?"

Jeevan thought for a few seconds before he replied, "I was wondering about how if Raghuvir would take a bit of responsibility for his workers, there were so many ways in which they could be helped."

He then went on to explain how the workers didn't get their wages on time, and the lack of proper water, toilet and even medical facilities on the compound caused major inconveniences from time to time.

"So many things could be changed if only someone took the initiative," he rued.

Satya had been listening patiently all this while. He felt his admiration for his friend grow even stronger as he started to see Jeevan in a new light. The way this young man thought was more progressive than most of the educated people out there. Satya felt that with proper guidance and help Jeevan might actually be able to make a difference for the workers.

The two men walked down a small alley which happened to be a shortcut to the slum. It was a bit desolate and away from the commotion of the busy streets. Jeevan noticed a group of men sitting at the far end of the alley, underneath a tree, along with bottles containing a yellow-coloured liquid and motorcycles surrounding them. The group consisted of merely three or four men but the noise of their screaming and shouting could be heard from a distance, such was the level of their intoxication. Satya grabbed Jeevan's arm and pulled, asking him to stop. Jeevan turned around to see a worried look on his friend's face and asked him about it.

"Let's not go from here," said Satya, in a calm but serious tone.

"But why *dada*, I'm not scared," replied Jeevan, puffing his chest out a little jokingly.

"You are a fool not to be," said Satya before he pulled him abruptly and started walking in the opposite direction.

Jeevan was a bit shaken to be on the receiving end of this kind of unexpected behaviour from his friend. Satya noticed the disturbed look on his face and sighed loudly.

He put his hand on Jeevan's shoulder and said, "You're new here, my friend. You don't know certain things the way I do. That's why you should listen to the advice I give you."

Jeevan didn't seem convinced. He looked at Satya and asked, "What do you mean?"

Satya looked at Jeevan and thought for a while, almost hesitating, before he said, "Life hasn't been particularly easy for me as well, my friend. Since I've arrived here, I have faced hardships at every corner."

Satya then went on to tell Jeevan how he had been bullied by a similar group of drunk men in his early days. They were a group of five and had approached him to ask for a lighter. This was before they realised that he did not speak their language and belonged to a different state. In their intoxicated state, they had made fun of Satya's accent.

He had tried to walk away from the conversation in response to their bullying. The group had gotten physical following which one of them had stabbed him in the shoulder with a broken piece of glass before taking off.

"I still bear the mark from that day," said Satya, pulling down a part of his shirt, revealing an ugly scar on the tip of his shoulder blade.

Jeevan stared at him for a while, his thoughts spiralling in his head. He had no idea how to respond to what Satya had just told him. He had led a simple life from the very beginning. He belonged to a remote village where physical violence of this level was a rare occurrence. So, for him, getting attacked like this for no apparent reason made zero sense. As a matter of fact, he had trouble believing what he was hearing till Satya showed him his injury from the assault.

"Life here is not as simple as it used to be back at home, my friend. People here are different, they have selfish needs and perverted thoughts. You need to be careful so that no one takes advantage of your good nature."

Satya had a different air about him now, which made Jeevan realise that he was being dead serious. This was only the second time they were meeting but he hadn't seen this side of Satya before.

"I understand, *dada,*" he replied. Satya's face softened instantly.

As they approached the main street, Satya said, "I'll see you next month," as he raised his hand to stop a passing auto rickshaw. He left a slightly disturbed Jeevan, standing in the darkness of the night.

CHAPTER 11

PREPARATION

It was almost nine by the time Jeevan reached home. The yard would be closed the next day so the slum was maximally occupied. Several workers and their wives were still up and about, a scene uncommon for Jeevan at this time of the night.

"Oi, Jeevan," came a loud voice from behind him.

He turned around to look at Aman and a few of his friends sitting under a tree with glasses full of alcohol in their hands. All these workers, including Aman, had shifted to this slum recently after they got assigned to work at the same yard as Jeevan. His commute to and from the yard had become less boring ever since.

An instant feeling of discomfort washed over Jeevan as he stood there unsure of his next course of action. Aman called out to him again before he jogged his way across to Jeevan, half singing, half dancing, clearly not in complete control of his senses.

"*Kahan se aa raha hai?* Where have you been?" Aman asked him, a childish grin on his face as he pranced around, unable to stand still in one spot.

Jeevan did not wish to engage in a conversation with Aman when he was in an intoxicated state, especially after the things he had heard from Satya just a while ago. But he also did not have the heart to turn down one of the few friends that he had.

"*Ladki ke saath tha kya?* Were you out with a girl?" asked Aman once more before he burst out laughing.

Jeevan tried to deny it, but his attempt failed. For some reason, Aman had decided to believe that he had been out with a girl. He suddenly stopped laughing and tried to make a very serious face which was almost comical considering how drunk he was. He put his arms around Jeevan's shoulders and came really close to him, his reeking breath evidence of all the alcohol he had consumed.

"You are my friend, Jeevan. It is my duty to tell you to be careful of the sickness that they can give you," Aman stuttered, managing to complete the sentence after two failed attempts.

"Sickness? What sickness?" Jeevan had a confused look on his face.

"They call it AIDS or something. It's what you get when you lay with one of those girls," Aman's speech was getting difficult to comprehend now.

Jeevan realised that it was futile trying to converse with him and said, "Come, brother, you have had a lot to drink. You should get some rest."

Jeevan wrapped his arms around Aman, supporting his weight as he slowly walked him over to his hut and helped him lie down on his bed.

Jeevan looked around as if searching for something before he asked Aman, "Don't you have any blankets?"

A loud grunt was his reply and he turned around to see Aman fast asleep with his mouth wide open. Jeevan smiled a little before he walked out the door and returned to his own hut. The commotion outside had still not completely died down as Jeevan saw a group of middle-aged men dancing around each other. There were no women or children in sight and given the situation, he could understand why.

He made his way back to his hut where he put his belongings on the bed and pulled out the same pouch that always remained tied around his waist. He then untied the strings of the pouch which now looked a bit saggy and heavy and overturned the entire thing on his bed. The numerous coins that fell out of the pouch along with paper notes made a very audible noise, louder than Jeevan would have liked. He turned and walked towards the door, peeking out to make sure no one was around to see him with the money. After finally overcoming his paranoia, he walked back to his bed, sat down and started counting the money scattered on it.

"Three thousand two hundred fifty-five, six, seven…"

Jeevan finished counting as he placed six more coins on top of the pile. He felt proud for having earned this much money all on his own. But there was a part of him which was angry. He knew he deserved to have more money with him. Since they were paid on a daily wage basis, Raghuvir was supposed to hand them their money regularly, every evening at the end of the day. But he had not been coming to the yard ever since the gang showed up threatening to kill him. So that had left all the workers, including Jeevan no choice but to keep working without getting paid for almost a week, in the hope that they would get all of it back once Raghuvir returned.

Jeevan took the money, neatly folded the notes and put the bundle inside the pouch again, followed by the coins as he tied it firmly with the string to his waist. He wanted to send some money to his family but had no idea how to. He started doing some calculations in his head.

Jeevan's facial expression changed by the second as he continued doing the math in his head as to how much he would need to go on for a while. His smile was slowly wiped off his face as he got up and went to check for supplies within the house. He realised that after purchasing the necessary groceries and other things for the week, he won't have enough to send back home. Guilt washed over him as he once again felt helpless, not being able to take responsibility for his family.

A solitary tear ran down his cheek as Jeevan suddenly felt anger well up within him, recalling a particular person. It was not long before he was seething with fury, blaming his family's condition on Raghuvir. His thoughts took him back to earlier that evening when he was with Satya. He remembered asking Satya about the supervisory position but their conversation had been cut short. Jeevan's thoughts started following the same track again. He wondered about how he could help all the workers from a position of power like that.

A loud whistling sound dragged him back into reality. It was the noise of a pressure cooker from someone's hut within the slum that had disrupted the silence in the air. Jeevan took a deep breath, regaining his composure as he was reminded that he still had to make dinner arrangements. He had an outing planned for the next day. He wanted to walk around the city and explore it, something he hadn't gotten a proper chance to do ever since his arrival. A slight excitement found its way through the anger and sorrow as he sat down to prepare for the next day.

CHAPTER 12

A SMALL GETAWAY

Jeevan started early the next day, enjoying the cool morning breeze as he walked down the road. The sea looked astoundingly beautiful as it reflected the yellow rays of the morning sun and gentle waves slowly crashed on the beach. There were several people on the beach, some jogging and some exercising. There was a group of teenagers clicking photos and a lot of hawkers selling a variety of things. Everything about the setting was normal but Jeevan didn't know why it made him sad. He had never seen the ocean before coming to Gujarat and ever since he laid his eyes on the horizon, he had been in love with it. Not a single day had passed since his arrival wherein Jeevan had not spent at least a few minutes of his day staring out at the sea and letting his emotions free for a while.

The yard was situated right next to the shore so he had the time to just stand and think, and address his mental conflicts. But the past few days had been different. Whenever he approached the sea, he would be overcome with sadness and guilt as his thoughts, through no control of his own, took him back to his family. Even the nightmare was beginning to feel more real as the days passed, so Jeevan made less frequent visits to the beach.

There was a restaurant with a big balcony facing the sea, across the road from where Jeevan was standing. He looked at the big shining logo, decorated with a lot of lights.

It said something in English that he did not understand and assumed that it was the name of the restaurant. He saw numerous cars parked in front of the restaurant and the balcony was filled with people, mostly parents with their kids and couples who had come for breakfast while enjoying the magnificent view. Jeevan hadn't had anything to eat since that morning but he knew that the place would be expensive.

Regardless of that, ignoring his instincts which asked him to back away, he approached the restaurant's front door. There was a small table beside the entrance and behind it stood a well-dressed man with a black notebook in his hand. Upon noticing Jeevan, the smile on the man's face turned into a scowl as he approached and asked him in English, "Can I help you?"

Jeevan looked confused. He neither understood nor knew how to speak the language. He stood there for a while, staring at the man before he said, "*Chai*?" asking if they served tea.

The man let out a frustrated sigh and said in Hindi, "Yes we serve *chai*, it is 150 rupees."

The man noticed how Jeevan's eyes had widened and his facial expression had changed after hearing the price of the tea.

He burst out laughing, and inconsiderately said, "What were you thinking? Poor people like you can't afford to eat at places like these."

Jeevan turned around and started walking in the opposite direction, feeling ashamed. He kept walking till the restaurant and the man went out of sight. Suddenly he saw an old man, sitting on the footpath with a small tea stall right there on the pavement. The arrangement was simple. The old man had a small gas cylinder which powered a very small stove. The stove was placed on a crate which had a big hole in the middle allowing the pipe from the cylinder, which was placed under the crate, to connect to the stove. Next to the stove, were numerous clay cups, something very common back in West Bengal.

Jeevan approached the man and politely asked, "*Dada, chai?*"

The old man's face lit up with a smile. He asked Jeevan to sit and lit the stove. Jeevan looked behind the stall to see a few plastic stools placed on the pavement. A small signboard hung from a tree trunk beside the stall which had something written on it in Hindi.

"*Chai, Small – Five rupees, Big – Ten rupees,*" read Jeevan silently. He then turned to the old man and said, "Small *chai, dada.*"

The old man nodded and busily stirred the mixture again as he hummed a tune. Jeevan suddenly realised that there were no other customers. He looked around to see if there were any other tea stalls around but there were none.

"*Babu,* here is your *chai,*" said the old man suddenly, holding a tray in his hand which had a cup of tea in it.

Jeevan took the steaming cup and blew on it lightly a few times before taking a small sip. His eyes lit up upon tasting the perfect blend of tea leaves and milk. The tea was freshly prepared and steaming hot but it did not take Jeevan too long to finish the entire thing. He got up and paid the man the five rupees, thanking him for the tea before resuming his journey.

It was almost ten in the morning and Jeevan was walking, but his mind was engaged elsewhere. He had been wondering about something for quite some time but didn't know how to solve the issue. The big restaurant despite being very expensive and having such rude employees had many customers. On the other hand, the old man, who treated his customers with such kindness and sold tea at such a low price had no takers. The fact that his tea had such an amazing taste made the matter all the more illogical for Jeevan. He could not come up with a single reason to explain this difference.

Jeevan had entered a different area by now. It was considerably more developed than the part of the city he lived in. The buildings had started increasing in height and there were some as tall as twenty storeys. Jeevan felt as if he had entered a different city, the change was so huge and so abrupt. Many more buses and cars were running on the road now and the city-like commotion was back but in a much more disciplined fashion. The cars were not honking as much, bikers wore helmets, and all the cars and even the people behaved civilly, unlike the main street in front of his slum where there were fights and yelling amongst drivers and pedestrians almost every day.

He walked down a clean, concrete pavement lined with snack stalls. They were properly made and decorated unlike the thatched stalls back in his area. The road was long and seemed to keep going as he continued down the path. There was one thing that bothered Jeevan a lot though. Cars and buses were passing by him every single moment and every other vehicle left behind a black film of smoke from its exhaust. This smoke slowly accumulated and, in turn, rose to combine with the air creating a smoky and suffocating atmosphere.

He was taken back to the very first day of his arrival when he had seen a huge banner, with people speaking loudly over loudspeakers, addressing the issues of pollution and global warming. He had taken a few minutes to stand and listen to them talk about similar issues of exhaust from cars and motorcycles due to irregular maintenance. It caused a decline in the engine's function. This produced more harmful toxins upon combustion, which escaped via the exhaust and were released into the atmosphere. This had accumulated over the years and had apparently made the planet much hotter. There were several other examples that they had spoken about, but Jeevan specifically remembered this.

There were buildings everywhere, making it impossible for any fresh air to pass through properly. The small plots which were empty either had cars parked in them or were occupied by small bazaars. Jeevan passed the entrance of an immense compound which had about four or five buildings within it. The gates were open and there was a huge queue of cars in front of it, stretching down to the main road. It took Jeevan a couple of minutes to reach the entrance by which time the queue hadn't moved at all.

He noticed a big red plus sign with something written below it in English. He realised that it was a hospital. The compound was immense and the infrastructure made it look like a luxury hotel. Jeevan noticed a parking sign beside the entrance with a fee of 'thirty rupees per hour' written on it in bold letters. Jeevan silently crossed the hospital and continued walking down the street until he decided to take a left along one of the narrower streets to get away from the bustle and suffocation.

The change was again very abrupt as within a couple of minutes of walking the bustle died down and the streets got narrower. They were now divided by a narrow concrete slab in between, which stretched down the road. A variety of trees and shrubs grew on the slab making the road look very beautiful. There were houses as far as the eye could see on both sides of the street. Some were small, some big, some so luxurious looking on the outside that Jeevan could only imagine what the inside must be like. He saw a milk van stop and deliver packets of milk to every house down the lane, one after another.

A familiar sorrow overtook Jeevan. He was reminded of how basic his life was. Milk was a luxury and there was no proper water supply to his hut or any other hut in their slum for that matter. There was a tube well in their slum which provided water twice a day. He had to wake up every morning to stand in line with countless other men and women and await his turn to collect water. He was taken back to a few minutes ago when he noticed the parking board outside the hospital.

"Let only the treatment be considered. Why are they charging so much to keep your car while you attend to a sick person?" he thought disgustedly.

CHAPTER 13

MAKING A
MISTAKE

It was seven in the evening and it had been quite some time since sunset. The screws made a rattling noise as the bus roared its way down the road, almost sounding like the engine was going to give out. Jeevan stared out the window, a childish excitement in his eyes as he watched the cars and motorcycles race by. Every experience was a new one for him. He hadn't really gotten the chance to travel too much since the majority of his school life included walking two kilometres every day.

Jeevan had spent the rest of the day walking around the same area. He had packed a meal of lentils and rice so that he could save money on food. It was not until around four in the evening, on his way back, that he noticed the huge bus depot with numerous buses parked inside. He had expected the fare to be high and was reluctant to approach the huge ticket counter but curiosity got the better of him. He got in line behind four other people and patiently waited for his turn.

"*Kidhar?*" questioned the woman behind the desk, asking him where he wanted to go.

"Ramnagar," Jeevan replied timidly, expecting to be slapped with an outrageous price.

"Eight rupees."

Jeevan's joy knew no bounds as he confirmed the price and happily paid the fare, making his way towards the small, brown-coloured bus which was half-full. Back in his village, they had to wait for several minutes on the main road before a bus came along to take them to their destination. It was not possible to get a seat on those buses as they would already be occupied by people who had boarded the bus earlier. The fact that there were so many buses, waiting for people to board them and not the other way around, was very fascinating to him.

The bus halted at a big junction where more people boarded it. Jeevan suddenly heard a few voices near him and saw a group of people pass by, dressed in sarees, a traditional Indian clothing item for women, but their voices were heavy and man-like. One of them branched off from the group and boarded the bus finally allowing Jeevan to take a good look at her face. The person had a big body structure, her arms and shoulders were far more muscular than a woman's body and she had visible facial hair. Jeevan had heard stories about eunuchs or *hijras* as the people around him used to call them. His work companions back at the slum had told him about them in detail a while ago.

"They like men more, you know?" one of them had told him, recalled Jeevan.

"I have heard they approach you and force you to do things," said another person.

"But aren't they males?" asked Aman.

"So what, I have heard of two men marrying, they can do it," came the reply.

Jeevan had listened to the conversation but had not participated but that was because he had not believed half of it.

The *hijra* approached Jeevan as he was sitting right by the door and clapped her hands twice before leaning on the door frame and asking him for money by saying, "*Dega, hero?*"

It was at this moment that a feeling of discomfort and fear gripped Jeevan. The phrase used by the person was simple but could be easily translated into sexual slang, something that the men at his slum did frequently. It was due to this misunderstanding that he misread the situation and frantically shook his head, instantly getting up and changing his seat. All eyes turned towards him as the person started saying something unpronounceable, clearly offended by his behaviour. Jeevan made his way to the back of the bus where he took another seat, knowing that others were still staring at him. He did not understand why people were frowning at him when the other person had tried to do something perverse to him, that too in front of everyone.

He suddenly heard the clapping of hands again and saw the *hijra* standing beside a man, leaning against the door frame, in the same way, with her palm stretched out. Jeevan almost felt a thunderbolt strike him as he saw the man place a solitary coin in her palm. She then blessed the man by placing her hand on his head, a symbol of blessing and prosperity. He continued to observe this as the person did the same thing with every person present on the bus, save the driver and ticket collector. Some gave coins, some gave notes but every person received the same blessing in return. The person slowly reached the end of the bus where Jeevan was seated but she did not approach him again. She turned around to get off the bus.

Jeevan put his head down and clenched his jaw, feeling a wave of guilt wash over him for having misjudged the person without being considerate. Once again, he had let his emotions get the better of him. He stared at the shaking floor of the bus and made a fist. The one-rupee coin which he had brought out after the incident in the hope of making amends with the person was now digging slowly into his skin as he clenched harder.

The distance that had taken him almost the entire day on foot took him less than two hours to travel by bus.

The streets started looking familiar as the traffic increased along with the honking and yelling. About ten minutes later the ticket collector yelled, "Ramnagar."

Jeevan walked towards the door as the bus halted at a dirty and smelly bus stop. He got off and turned around to see the familiar main street which he took every day while travelling to the yard. He then slowly made his way home, tiredness creeping up on all four limbs one by one. He thanked his stars for coming across the bus depot or it would have taken him a very long time to get back home. It took him ten more minutes to reach the slum by end of which his legs felt like they would stop working.

He had never walked as much in a single day before. He had to thank his excitement and curiosity for his long journey today. He entered the house and put his belongings down, repeating the process from last night. He then sat down on the bed to count the remaining money. Jeevan was growing increasingly paranoid with each passing day, as he had to carry the money everywhere with him due to the lack of proper storage space. He took a few minutes to count the money before putting the bundle back again. He made a mental note of the day's expenses, made the bed and lay down, his body too tired to make dinner despite the growing hunger inside him. The hunger did not bother him too much though, for his mind was busy elsewhere.

He was recalling the events of that day and a few things started bothering him again. He started wondering how misunderstood the *hijra* community really was, and the false information that people had about them, spoiling their reputation. Jeevan understood the feeling of being looked down upon and made to feel like an outcast all too well. He realised how the person on the bus might have felt and he couldn't forgive himself for behaving in such a way. He made up his mind that he would try and help raise awareness for the community to reduce harassment from ignorant people like himself.

He could not follow this thought process for too long though, as his fatigue got the better of him and a deep slumber overtook him.

CHAPTER 14

HONESTY OR GREED?

"**R**eally? What else did you see?" asked Darpana with a clear hint of excitement in her voice.

It had been a week since Jeevan's little getaway. He went to work the following day but did not get a chance to have a proper conversation with Darpana as both of them barely got free time after work. He had finally gotten the chance today as his shift ended a bit early and he didn't miss the opportunity to tell her about his experiences that day.

"I saw very big buildings, taller than all of these ships. I even saw a hospital which was bigger than this yard from the inside. I'm sure they can treat everything there," he continued cheerfully.

Darpana's face suddenly fell a little. The change was slight but enough for Jeevan to notice. He instantly stopped talking and stared at her, waiting for her to say something. Darpana was staring at the floor but the sudden silence made her look at Jeevan, her eyes glistening with tears. Jeevan didn't realise what had upset her till she started speaking again.

"Prakash, my husband," she said, a slight break in her voice.

A sudden realisation hit Jeevan as he was reminded of her husband's death, described by Aman quite some time ago. He looked away and stared out of the window, unsure of how to address this situation.

"He struggled for two whole hours in front of my eyes while they sat and did nothing," Darpana's voice grew colder as she continued. "I was told later that he had nine broken bones and a punctured lung. He had to endure all that pain and suffering before he died. All because of them."

Jeevan sat in complete silence and listened to her as she slowly gave voice to the emotions she had suppressed ever since the incident. She suddenly got up and walked to the end of the room where she opened a cabinet and pulled out a leather harness, torn in the middle where the safety belt was supposed to be.

She walked back and handed it to Jeevan saying, "This is what they gave him in exchange when he complained about faulty equipment."

Jeevan inspected the apparatus from top to bottom and his horror grew as the seconds passed. The harness was absolutely in no condition to worn as safety equipment. It was flimsy, torn in several places and looked at least half a decade old.

"I kept it so that I could show everybody but nobody could help. Even the healthcare facilities provided for us don't have the resources to treat big injuries. He might have been saved if we had taken him to a big hospital in time," she said as she sat down and started crying silently with tears running down her face.

Jeevan clutched the harness tightly, anger welling up inside him. There were a few minutes of silence between them as both of them stared in the same direction, but were engaged in very different kinds of thoughts. Darpana sat down with a broken expression, tiredness showing clearly on her face.

"Why didn't you go back?" asked Jeevan finally, deciding to break the silence with his question.

She looked at him, her eyes now devoid of any emotion and asked, "Go back where? Bihar? Where my own family married me off to get rid of me?"

Jeevan was a little taken aback at the sudden outburst. Darpana continued, her voice a little lower now, "They will never accept a widow. Neither my father nor my husband's family. So, I chose to stay here and start a new life for myself."

Darpana had noticed Jeevan's reaction to her outburst and it made her smile, lightening the mood a little.

"It hasn't been easy. You boys have occupied jobs in this industry all over the city so it was not easy to get a vacancy.

But we are just as good as you guys, that's how I managed to secure a job here," she shoved Jeevan with a playful and cheerful look on her face.

Jeevan noticed that the mood in the room had shifted and decided not to go back to the earlier conversation.

He looked at her and said, "I have been fascinated by ships from a very early age, so when I came across an opportunity to work in the industry, I couldn't let it go, no matter what." As he spoke his lips slowly arched into a sad smile. "It's not what I thought it would be like. I would actually like to move ahead and leave all of this behind someday."

A sudden knock on the door interrupted their conversation as a short man with a yellow cap and a big burly stomach walked in.

"Raghuvirji?"

Jeevan's eyes widened. This was the first time he was seeing Raghuvir since the gang incident and that had happened quite some time ago. Raghuvir also had a surprised look on his face as he stared at the two of them sitting next to each other.

"Hasn't your shift ended already?" asked Raghuvir, a confused and timid look on his face.

Darpana suddenly stood up and walked towards her bench, picked up a band-aid and looked back at Raghuvir to say, "He's hurt, he wanted medication. That's why he's here."

Jeevan looked at Darpana confusedly but quickly caught on to say, "Yes, I burnt my finger."

Raghuvir seemed uninterested as he was clearly in a hurry. He nodded his head and ran to the back of the room, taking a big key out and opening a cabinet which was usually locked.

He then fished for some documents for several minutes before Jeevan lost his patience and asked him, "Where have you been for so many days?"

The supervisor looked at Jeevan once before he picked up a few documents and locked the cabinet. He walked back towards them and said in a very low voice, "I'm sorry for the trouble I have caused. Please understand, if they find out they will kill me."

It had been quite some time since Jeevan had last seen Raghuvir, but looking at him now he couldn't recognise his supervisor anymore. His face had holes where his plump cheeks used to be, his eye sockets were black and swollen from an evident thrashing. He looked extremely tired and starved as he panted while talking.

"Here, take these, please," he said as he held out a few grey-coloured 500-rupee notes towards Jeevan. Jeevan's eyes were locked on Raghuvir's hands. The money was extremely tempting.

"Keep this. Share it between yourselves but please don't tell anyone that I was here. I will give the rest back very soon," the supervisor was almost begging at this point.

He approached Jeevan and stuffed the money in his hand, and left in a hurry. Jeevan stared at the money in his hands and felt a silent but intense joy creep up his spine giving him something like goosebumps all over his body. He counted ten notes in his hand which would mean two thousand five hundred rupees for each of them. That was more wage than a week's worth of work. He looked towards Darpana. His happiness was instantly wiped away when he noticed the clear disgust on her face.

"You realise that he bribed you, right? He gave you this money so that you keep quiet and take part in saving him from his wrongdoings," Darpana was clearly furious at him.

"But we can take this money and make things a bit easier. Neither of us has been paid in a while," Jeevan's smile was almost back on his face.

"Not we, only you. I will not take that money," she said as she stormed out of the room, leaving him staring with a helpless look on his face, unable to do anything.

CHAPTER 15

HELP

The alleyway was empty, the ground sloppy and slippery, as usual, but something about the scenario felt off. The narrow road felt hollow and hauntingly silent as Jeevan could hear his own footsteps, walking down the road. It was late in the evening, quite late because his shift had ended early today. He had spent all of this time talking to Darpana. It took him a few more minutes to get back home.

From the moment he had left the yard, he was deeply immersed in his thoughts, "I could send some of the money back home, to help them."

He thought of ways he could spend the money as he walked back. It was not a very big amount but it was more than enough for him. But the thought of Darpana kept bothering him throughout. It had been quite some time since he left the yard. As he was walking down the road, mumbling to himself, he saw a yellow auto-rickshaw rushing by. It stopped at the traffic signal about thirty feet away from him. Jeevan stared as he saw his supervisor climb out of the vehicle in a hurry before he scurried down the road. Jeevan started following him from a distance, bursting with curiosity.

After a couple of minutes, Raghuvir approached a worn-out, old building. He brought a key out from his pocket, unlocked the door and entered the house, closing the door behind him. Jeevan waited a few feet away from the three-storied building as if expecting something to happen. A few moments later, he turned around and made his way back again. By the time he reached home his conscience had finally overtaken his greed for the money as he realised how unfair it would be to his friends and the other workers.

He entered his hut and instantly dropped on his bed, his thoughts spiralling, "They would never forgive me if they came to know."

"How does it make me any different from Raghuvir if I become as greedy as he did? I left my family and friends behind for money once. I can't do it again."

Thoughts like these raced through his head as he closed his eyes in an attempt to pull himself out of them.

"Jeevan *bhai*," came a voice from outside.

Jeevan shot up, his hand instinctively going towards his waist as if to guard the money. A slight tapping on the wall was heard before Aman peeped in, looking at him with a playful grin on his face.

Jeevan's posture softened as he saw the familiar face and asked him, "*Kya chahiye?*"

He was curious to know what Aman wanted at this late hour. The two of them had developed a strong, ever-growing bond as they travelled to work together almost every day. Jeevan would help Aman out with his work both at the yard and at the slum whenever required and Aman returned the favour too. So, he had turned out to be one of Jeevan's most trusted companions.

"*Ladki?*" said Aman with a wink, hinting that Jeevan had been out with a girl again.

Jeevan did not respond gently and cheerfully, in the way that he usually did. It did not take Aman even a second to catch on that something was wrong.

He walked into the hut and sat on the floor in front of his friend and asked him, "*Kya hua bhai?*" in an attempt to figure out what was bothering him.

Jeevan sat and thought for a while before deciding to let Aman know about the entire thing. A few minutes later he brought out the money given by Raghuvir and said, "What do I do now? Will you help me out?"

Aman took the money and stared at it for a while before he took a deep breath in and said, "That is a lot to take in."

Jeevan nodded his head and waited patiently as Aman took a few more seconds to think before he started speaking again, "I understand Darpana's anger. I would be angry at you too."

He looked at Jeevan as he said this. "But that being said I also can't guarantee that I wouldn't have done the same had I been in your place. It's a lot of money and I have a tough family situation as well."

Aman had a clear look of guilt on his face. The burden of guilt that had been sitting like a rock on Jeevan's chest all this while instantly felt a little lighter.

"I'm glad that you didn't let your greed overtake you, my friend," said Aman, the relief evident in his voice.

Jeevan was still not completely out of it so he decided to lighten the mood a little. "Let's have dinner together today. I will help you cook," said Aman cheerfully.

Jeevan smiled a little at his friend's attempt to make him feel better. He complied and the two friends started making preparations for dinner. It was nearly ten at night when they finished cooking and sat down to eat.

Dinner was a simple dish of lentils, rice, potato curry and fried eggs which Aman brought from his house. It had been a hectic day but the two friends managed to turn it into a good night by talking and laughing amongst themselves, forgetting about the events of the day for some time. Though slight, the distraction on Jeevan's face showed. Aman decided to address the elephant in the room after nearly finishing their meal.

"I know what you're thinking about," he said, mouth still half full.

"What am I thinking about?" asked Jeevan in reply, in a slightly mocking tone.

"What will you do tomorrow? Will you return the money? Will you talk to Raghuvir?" continued Aman as he finished a glass full of water.

"You know me well, my friend. These questions have been bothering me for a while," said Jeevan with a faint smile.

"I would be lying if I said I wasn't thinking about it myself. After all none of us have been paid in a while. It's getting hard for everyone. But I thought of a way we might be able to take care of the problem."

Jeevan's face lit up with curiosity as he waited patiently for Aman to continue.

"Take the money and give it back to Raghuvir and ask him to pay all the workers their fair share. If he doesn't comply threaten him about ratting him out to the gang.

You know where he lives," said Aman in a half-serious tone, which made Jeevan wonder about his advice.

"What are you saying, Aman? I can't blackmail a person like this. Besides, I don't even know if that is his house or not. It might be some other place," replied Jeevan, trying to get the seemingly absurd idea out of his friend's head.

Aman ignored him and said, "You know as well as I do that it is his house. Also, you know that Raghuvir is not someone you can trust. He won't give us our money back on time if you don't do this. You have to help us, Jeevan."

Jeevan noticed Aman's eyes glistening slightly, almost as if he was about to cry. He got up abruptly, picked up the water jug and walked outside followed by Jeevan. The two washed their hands.

"My brother has been sick for a while now. I haven't been able to send any money this month and they don't have enough to buy medicines for him," said Aman, his voice breaking slightly.

The previously cheerful and mischievous expression was now replaced by that of sorrow, something that had been buried deep inside. Aman belonged to Gujarat but was from a different city, a name Jeevan didn't remember. But he did know that Aman's family came from a very poor background, possibly worse than his own. Aman had eight siblings, one of whom had passed away. The last one was very young and had been ill for some time now, something quite a few people in the yard were aware of.

Several emotions flooded Jeevan as he stood up and thought about the sheer number of workers suffering from the same fate, how they were working day after day without getting paid.

"All of this has to stop. I realise that and trust me when I say that it will stop. I'm just not sure that blackmailing someone is the right way to do it. Give me some time to think about this, Aman. I will talk to you tomorrow," said Jeevan, wanting to be left alone and stating it clearly.

"Sure, I trust you, my friend," Aman smiled weakly, dissatisfaction evident on his face before he turned around and started walking towards his hut.

"Aman," yelled Jeevan, making him turn back. "Thank you for today, *bhai,*" he said as he smiled widely.

CHAPTER 16

TRUCE

The sky was filled with greyish-black clouds as Jeevan walked silently down the road, deeply engaged in his thoughts. The previous night had passed with very little sleep as he kept repeating the things he would say to Raghuvir. He wasn't exactly the confrontational type. In fact, he was the exact opposite and had been like that for the majority of his life. But something about him had changed over time.

This time he wasn't feeling as scared as he usually did in situations like this. He had a feeling of being burdened and was nervous, but that was because he knew that he shouldered the responsibility of several other workers along with him today. He had not given Aman's suggestion much thought. But a part of him knew very well that the conversation might have to go down that path as Raghuvir was not the most rational or understanding person. It was known to all workers in the yard.

Ultimately, Jeevan had been unable to come up with a solution and decided to consult Darpana regarding this. He knew that she was upset with him and he wanted to make amends. Jeevan walked through the entrance as the noise of metal hitting metal grew louder with each step. He took a good look around the yard, the smoky film surrounding the area making it a little hard for him to see.

Jeevan coughed a few times and felt a weird itching in his throat as he made a loud sound in an attempt to clear any obstruction. This had been happening to him for a few days now. He suffered sudden bouts of coughing which would disappear as abruptly as they occurred. Jeevan made his way to the front office as he checked the list of workers for any change in duties. He was trying to figure out where Darpana was stationed today. Upon finding what he was looking for, he made his way across the yard, his nervousness slowly getting to him now.

He didn't know what to say to her or how to justify his behaviour. His fingers started feeling cold as he approached the door and saw her sitting on the bed, talking to some other woman, with a first aid box and an ointment in her hand, seemingly tending to an injury. He waited outside patiently for the next few minutes as they finished talking and the woman left the cabin. Darpana had walked up to the door with her and noticed Jeevan standing a few feet away, staring at the sea in the distance. Jeevan turned around on hearing her voice and instantly lowered his face to avoid eye contact, guilt slowly washing over him again.

"Come inside, I need to talk to you," she said before turning and going inside herself.

Jeevan followed her, his face gloomy, unsure of what to expect next.

"I'm sorry for behaving like that yesterday," said Darpana and Jeevan's head shot up. "I was angry and I directed it towards you, I shouldn't have done that."

The feeling of relief that replaced Jeevan's guilt on hearing this was unparalleled. He couldn't help but sigh as he said, "No you're right. It was my fault, I shouldn't have accepted the money. I will return it today and try to convince him to give back all the money he owes us."

He noticed the change in her expression as she looked visibly relieved. "But I need your help with something," said Jeevan as he walked into the room and placed his belongings down.

"I don't think that would be the right thing to do," said Darpana.

Jeevan had taken the last thirty minutes to explain how he might know where Raghuvir lives and the discussion he had with Aman. Darpana was also as reluctant as Jeevan in blackmailing the supervisor to get what they wanted. They sat beside each other as a cool breeze filled the air inside the room, making Darpana's untied hair flow and touch Jeevan's face, caressing his cheek. Jeevan, unable to control himself, breathed in deeply taking in the fragrance of her hair. His cheeks were now turning increasingly red.

"I have an idea. We can..." Darpana stopped mid-sentence as she noticed a half-distracted Jeevan staring at her dreamily, and smiling slightly.

She giggled and cleared her throat, making him snap back to reality as she continued, "So as I was saying, I have a different idea to deal with this."

Jeevan was flustered as he tried to say something but ended up stuttering, making it difficult for her to understand. Darpana laughed loudly, not being able to hold it in any longer and Jeevan ended up smiling as well.

After a moment, Darpana started again, "So as I was saying, instead of blackmailing him, what if we tried to make a truce with him? Get on his good side. That way we can help the other workers in the future as well if any problem were to happen."

Jeevan's eyes lit up. It sounded like a very good idea to him as it did not involve any violence or blackmailing.

"But how do I do that? He doesn't like me and I don't trust him as well," said Jeevan, looking troubled.

On hearing this, Darpana breathed in, got up and looked out, checking if anyone could hear them and then closed the door. She then walked back to Jeevan who was clearly very confused.

"What I'm about to tell you can't leave this room. I'm trusting you with this information," said Darpana, looking serious.

Jeevan realised that she was not joking around and nodded politely as she continued, "Raghuvir might not be here for very long. I have rotating shifts so I have access to the office as well. Raghuvir dropped off some documents some time ago, at the office, after the incident. I couldn't make out most of it since it was written in English, but I'm pretty positive that it was a document requesting a transfer."

Jeevan's eyes widened as he slowly realised what Darpana was hinting at. "He's so scared that he wants to leave his job at the yard? You're right! It will be easy to get the money out of him if he's in a state now."

Darpana smacked her palm on her forehead, exhibiting frustration. "That is not what I was getting to, at all. You're a simple and silly person," she said, smiling slowly, "That is why I trust you with this. Because you have a good heart and you want to help the people around you."

Jeevan still wore a confused expression as Darpana explained, "If Raghuvir is gone, we'll have an opening for the supervisor position. What if you applied for that position? You'd have the power to make a difference and you could help the workers get out of further miseries if they were to face any."

There were a few moments of silence before Jeevan got up and walked towards the table. He picked up the jug of water and drank from it for as long as it took to digest whatever Darpana had just told him.

"Supervisor? Me?"

His mind was racing at this point. Truth be told, it's not like the thought of Raghuvir being replaced by someone else had not crossed his mind but he never imagined himself in that position. He thought he lacked the expertise, the education and the leadership qualities required to take up such a huge responsibility.

"How can I become the supervisor? I know nothing about the job except gas cutting. I don't even know how to speak English," Jeevan asked her.

"Do you think Raghuvir knows how to speak English? He's good for nothing who wastes his time as the…"

Darpana was interrupted by a sudden uproar outside. The two of them looked at each other before rushing out of the cabin. They noticed a huge gathering on the other side of the yard. They walked over to the crowd and reached its centre. They heard someone calling out names rather loudly. Raghuvir sat at the very centre as he called out names and handed out envelopes to the workers.

Jeevan looked around to see a few of them open the envelopes filled with money. It took them quite some time to get through the entire group by the end of which the majority of the crowd had dispersed, save a few who were looking for answers. But before they could ask anything, Raghuvir got up and made his way out of the yard hurriedly, leaving all of them wondering about what had just happened.

The overall atmosphere of the yard improved considerably, as by the end of the day the workers knew that they could go home knowing they wouldn't have to sleep on an empty stomach. Jeevan stared at the envelope in his hand as he sat by his equipment, throat itchy and eyes tired after a full day of work. He was sitting atop the tallest ship in the yard, some twenty feet above the ground as he absent-mindedly stared at the expanse of the yard below him. He hadn't gotten a chance to talk to Darpana since she had been called away for some work shortly after the supervisor left and hadn't returned since.

Jeevan wanted to finish the conversation he had been having with her as more and more questions about the plan she had come up with, were adding to the already massive pile inside his head. A man walked by, right underneath

Jeevan, white envelope in hand and humming a joyful tune, clearly overjoyed at receiving his hard-earned money.

Kamal. Jeevan knew the man. They had worked together for almost a week before he was shifted to another part of the yard. Kamal had a sick wife with a lump in her chest. He had been working at the yard for two years now, struggling every single day to make ends meet. Jeevan took a moment to look around and get a glimpse of the faces around him. The faces he worked with every day, but something about them was different. He saw sickness and tragedy everywhere his eyes landed as he struggled to find one person who was not suffering from any kind of trauma, physical or otherwise. Giving them their wage was the bare minimum Raghuvir could do and yet the fulfilment of that bare minimum task brought happiness to so many individuals.

His eyes fell on another familiar face amongst the others, this one more familiar than the rest. He had a big smile on his face as he slowly picked up his equipment, an audible song on his lips. Aman had a sick brother on the verge of death and still, here he sat, strong enough to enjoy the little things in life. Jeevan realised how much he envied Aman to be able to do that. They had begun to feel like his family and the happiness on their faces gave Jeevan a certain satisfaction. He had started feeling responsible for the well-being of these people.

"I can help them. I know I can," smiled Jeevan, the evening sun casting a warm glow on his tired face.

CHAPTER 17

LETTER FROM HOME

"The truck then leaves for the steel industry where the metal is processed," explained Darpana to Jeevan as she held a small black notebook in her hand. It was after work hours and the sun had almost set, giving the evening sky an orange hue.

The duo sat beside each other in the same cabin as Darpana helped Jeevan understand how the yard functioned. It had been a few months since they started doing this, ever since Jeevan had decided to help the workers to get their rights. Darpana had been a huge help as she had experience working in almost all sectors of the yard. Additionally, she possessed Prakash's, her late husband's, notebook which had detailed descriptions of every corner of the yard and the functions carried out within. Prakash had been working at the yard for quite some time before the accident and according to Darpana, had always had a fascination for the yard. He dedicated years of research and struggle to put this small diary together, in the hope that one day when he got his promotion, he'd be well prepared for it. This diary was the reason why Darpana was so skilled at her work and seemed to have an idea about everything going on in the yard.

Jeevan had come to know about a lot of things he had been previously ignorant about thanks to her help. The bond between the two had grown deeper over time and they had become quite fond of each other now. People around often frowned over the age gap between them but that seldom bothered Jeevan. They had not talked about it amongst each other though. The subtle eye contact and flirtatious grins from both sides were the only attempts made to try and push it forward. Fear was holding them back. Darpana was afraid of the things people would say about a widow getting into a new relationship with a younger man and Jeevan was afraid of the mental impact the societal pressure would put on her, forcing both of them to refrain from expressing their feelings.

He had come a long way in a short span of time, though. He now understood the functioning of the yard to an extent where he could help the supervisor carry out certain duties. Raghuvir had been mostly absent following the refusal of his transfer request, allowing Jeevan to take advantage of the situation. For the past few months, with Darpana's help, he had managed to get on the 'good side' of the supervisor. The goons had returned along with the young boy a few weeks ago but Jeevan handled the entire situation by convincing Raghuvir to give them some money. They then decided to leave, promising to let the entire incident go. Jeevan felt guilty for letting Raghuvir off the hook so easily but he knew that it was necessary.

Following the incident, Raghuvir developed a liking for Jeevan and began trusting him with responsibilities around the yard. Initially, Jeevan had very little idea of what to do but with Darpana by his side, the two of them started overcoming the obstacles one after the other. Thanks to his efforts, the workers received their wages on time now which ultimately resulted in resolving quite a few conflicts in the yard.

"Do you know how important this industry is for the country?" Darpana asked Jeevan. Jeevan looked up at her, hesitation kicking in as the question was not expected.

"It helps the economy," he stuttered, remembering his conversation with Satya, months ago.

Darpana smiled slightly, clearly impressed at the response as she said, "Yes, but there are other things. It helps provide opportunities to thousands of men and women like us, who would remain unemployed otherwise."

She closed the notebook and placed it on the bed as she continued, "When the two of us first came here, we had no money and no shelter. I did not want to come but Prakash had forced me to, assuring me that we would have a better life here. We were living on the streets for a while before he got a chance to work here and our lives did change, but only for a while."

A sad smile appeared on her face. Jeevan was just about to say something when he felt the words get stuck in his throat and he burst out coughing. The bout went on for a few minutes. Darpana offered him some water, which he drank viciously. By the time the coughing stopped completely, his eyes were bloodshot and the vessels in his arms had popped up due to the stress. Darpana looked worried as Jeevan had been having coughing bouts like this for a few days now. She had asked him to go see a doctor but he had insisted that he had no time to spare. Jeevan drank some more water before he finally felt a little better.

Jeevan finally left the yard after another hour, a smile on his face as he slowly made his way back home, his thoughts keeping him company. He reached around his back to pull out a piece of paper, folded in two. He closed his eyes for a moment, the contents of the letter flashing before his eyes as clear as day.

He proceeded to open the letter and silently read the paragraph written in Bengali, "Greetings Jeevan, hope you're doing well. We have received your money and are thankful to you for it. But when are you coming back? Mother has changed since you left and won't talk much. I know you think she's angry with you and she says you will change and become different but I know she misses you. So do I. She has been sicker than usual since we haven't been able to give her the medication for a while. But we have got it now thanks to your help and hopefully, she will feel better again. Bhoomi *didi* visited a while ago but she was sad and said that she will be leaving soon. She was asking for you. Everybody misses you. Hope to see you soon, *bhaiya.*"

The letter was from his younger brother, Krishna. Jeevan had received this letter some time ago and had read it countless times. He had finally figured out how to send money back home and had been doing it for a while before he received this letter. The white envelope had brought a reality check along with it. The news about Bhoomi was heartbreaking in itself. The feeling was further fuelled when Jeevan realised why his family had not been able to afford his mother's medication for a while. He had left his village with all the money they had, leaving them completely broke. He had no idea how they had gotten by over the next few days, something he had forgotten to consider during all these months. The realisation was heartbreaking.

Jeevan had finished school a little later than the rest but that was the end of his education for him. His father died of a 'disease in his chest' as termed by the local doctors, who did not have the means to treat his father in the village. His family neither had the money nor the support to take his father to one of the big cities for treatment. So, the entire family watched for two months straight as the man inched towards death.

After his father died, the family's responsibility fell on Jeevan's shoulders. His mother had a severe asthma problem but she did everything possible, to keep the family running. She used to work as a maid for other houses in the village, cooked at small gatherings and even stitched garments at times for others, all to earn some money for her family. Jeevan had mostly worked small jobs like assisting shopkeepers at the village market. No one was ready to employ such a young child. Jeevan had spent the last few years watching his mother day and night but never once did she allow them to miss meals. When times were too bad, she would feed the children, even if it were just water and rice, and go hungry herself. She would prefer buying small things for his siblings over her own medicines. Such was his mother.

"And look what I did to her," his eyes glistened as he thought about her.

He always wondered why his mother would not work at a job where she would get more money for the work she did, some daily wage job like he did now. But now he knew why. He had done a head count, just out of curiosity, to see how many women got the opportunity to work in the industry. His shock was inexpressible. Almost ninety-five per cent of the workers were men. There were, in fact, no female gas cutters. The job is too hard for a woman, they said. But he had experienced how strong a woman can be. Jeevan made a silent promise to himself that he would go back home in a few months to meet his family.

Jeevan opened the lock on the newly installed door of his hut. Things had been looking up for him recently and he had made a few changes to his home. He had installed a door and a lock for safety purposes along with new utensils and kitchenware. He walked in and locked the door behind him. There was some sort of a gathering outside but Jeevan was too tired to pay attention to any of that. He was supposed to meet Satya tomorrow. They had met a few times in the last few months but only for exchanging money. Both of them had been pretty busy and it was Satya who had approached him with the idea of meeting on a holiday.

Satya had been a huge source of support for him, something he reminded himself of time and again. He had helped Jeevan transfer money to his family, a thing which he had found impossible to do on his own. He had also helped Jeevan with the post office formalities. This allowed him to exchange letters with his family. And as if all of this wasn't enough, he had promised to help Jeevan learn the

English language, so that he would be able to understand certain things much better. He felt a familiar sense of joy for having such good friends in his life. He finished his food and stood up, proceeding to wash his dishes as he was suddenly interrupted by a knock on the door.

CHAPTER 18

A FRIEND INDEED

"*Kaun?*" asked Jeevan cautiously as company at this time of the night usually never brought good news with it.

"It's me, Aman," came the reply from the other side. Jeevan's eyes widened. "Aman?"

Ever since Jeevan had helped Raghuvir get out of trouble with the gang, a few of the workers had expressed their dissatisfaction over the incident quite vocally. Aman had been one of them. Naturally, the bond between them had become shaky as their interactions were less frequent. Also, Jeevan's lessons with Darpana after work were a secret. So the two friends had stopped commuting to and from work together as well. Emotions regarding this situation had given rise to conflicts within Jeevan's mind quite a few times but he had remained strong so as to not give in to those emotions. He had tried making amends but Aman had proved to be a very stubborn and unreasonable person, showing a side that Jeevan didn't know existed.

They still conversed from time to time, but it was strictly professional. So, to see him at his door, at this time of the night was quite a surprise for Jeevan. He opened the door to see a crying Aman, reeking of alcohol, walk towards him and embrace him tightly as he continued to sob. For a few moments, Jeevan didn't know how to react. When he finally came to his senses, he dragged Aman inside and made him sit on the bed, hastily getting him a glass of water to drink.

"Are you okay, Aman? *Kya hua, bhai?*" he asked Aman if everything was okay, addressing him as a brother as he used to before.

"Everything is over, how am I supposed to be okay?"

His crying made it very hard to interpret what he was saying, and he continued, "My brother is very sick and he probably won't make it past the week."

Jeevan was overwhelmed with sorrow as his friend continued, "He had asked me to come home soon. I had promised him I would make enough money and return to make him all better. I couldn't, and he just kept getting worse," Aman's howling had stopped but his tears hadn't. "I don't have the money for his treatment, I don't know what to do now. My little brother will die, Jeevan."

Jeevan sat and thought for a while as the face of his own brother and his letter flashed in front of his eyes. He knew what it was like to have a sibling and the fear of losing them. It was unbearable. It did not take Jeevan much time to decide on what to do next. He got up and walked towards a big clay piggy bank that he kept hidden under his bed. This was one of the main reasons why he got the door installed. He broke the piggy bank in front of Aman. A loud cracking noise was heard, following a distinctive jingling and rattling as a huge number of coins and notes fell out of the broken clay pot. Jeevan gathered all the notes and took a few minutes to count them before handing them to Aman.

"Here is eleven thousand rupees. Take this and send it home for your brother's treatment. I hope this helps," said Jeevan in a very humble voice.

Aman's expression changed to one of shock, "I can't Jeevan, what are you saying? You also have a sick mother to support. I can't possibly take this." He shook his head vigorously, his drunken state almost making him lose balance.

"I have already sent money home this week. Besides, I will receive our wages, so I'll have money soon. You can repay me when you have the money but for now, concentrate on your brother's health. I have Krishna, so I know what it's like. I just wish I could help more," said Jeevan sadly.

Aman took the bundle of notes, disbelief written clearly on his face as he turned it over and over, almost as if he was unable to believe that the money was real.

He then turned towards Jeevan, eyes filled with gratitude as he said, "I will pay you as soon as I can, my friend.

You don't know what you have done for me, I will never forget this."

Aman then got up, barely able to stand straight. He struggled out of the tent, a sway in his step. Jeevan offered to help him walk back to his hut but he strictly declined by insisting, "I am fine. You have already done enough, Jeevan. I can do the rest on my own, my friend."

Jeevan didn't want to agitate him further so he let him walk back on his own, following him closely. Aman was too intoxicated to notice him. After Aman had entered his hut and Jeevan was satisfied, he turned around to walk back home. He smiled a smile which expressed his happiness at being able to support a close friend in a time of need but at the same time, he felt a distinctive chill along his spine. He could quite place a finger on the source of the feeling.

CHAPTER 19

DECEIT

"Get the information and let me know if the truck has reached on time," said Jeevan absent-mindedly as he flipped the pages of the document in front of him.

"Anything else, *bhaiya?*" the man asked.

Jeevan shook his head to reply in the negative to his question. The man turned around and was just about to leave when Jeevan called after him and asked, "*Achha suno.*"

The man stopped and turned around, waiting patiently for Jeevan to make his request. "Have you heard anything from Aman yet?" Jeevan asked and got the same answer he had gotten the last four times he had asked, over the last two months.

The morning after that conversation with Aman had been pretty uneventful and awfully similar to Jeevan's daily routine as he got up early and went to work. It was a holiday for the workers and yet he had some work assigned to him by the supervisor that he had to take care of, before meeting Satya and spending the rest of the day catching up with him. The duo spent some quality time together, where Satya continued his English lessons with Jeevan. He tried telling Satya about the progress he had been making at the yard in English. Throughout the conversation, Satya sat patiently and corrected his errors, grammatical or otherwise. He was clearly having a very hard time but was making steady progress.

All was going well until he told Satya about the money he had lent Aman. Jeevan saw the expression on Satya's face change to a worrisome frown which replaced the previously cheerful expression.

"What happened, Satya?" he asked, still not being able to understand the reason.

Satya looked back at him and once again his frown turned into a slight smile, a helpless smile at the naiveness of his dear friend. He did not want to get wrong and miscalculated ideas inside Jeevan's head so he chose not to address the topic. Satya shook his head and forced a big grin on his face as he attempted to change the topic. Jeevan noticed the weird change in Satya's behaviour but decided to let it go, but a small part of him was bothered for the rest of the evening.

It was not very late when Jeevan started for home. The day had been a very pleasant one, so pleasant in fact that he had forgotten about the events of last night. He walked down the sidewalk, constantly rehearsing the English alphabet and his vocabulary mentally, in an attempt to get rid of his obvious accent. He was going over the conversations he had with Satya, making a mental note of the corrections made by his friend when he thought about the weird interaction with him about the money. He picked up his pace as a sudden panic gripped his heart.

"That can't be the reason why, right?" he kept asking himself, trying to keep his optimism intact as he sped back home.

It had been almost two months since then. The other workers had told him that Aman had left that morning, an hour after him. He was carrying his belongings and had told the rest of them that he had to go back home on an urgent basis, leaving no contact details or even a message for Jeevan behind. For a while, Jeevan didn't let his paranoia get the better of him. He convinced himself that Aman had gone back to take care of his sick brother and would be back soon. But as the days flew by, so did his trust in his friend's honesty.

He finally decided to search the records of the workers for the contact details of his village. Darpana had been a huge help to him in this. The two of them finally found a number listed under Aman's father's name. It took around ten minutes for Jeevan to knock the remaining doubt out of his head as he came to know that Aman's brother had passed away quite some time ago. Aman had left and not returned since.

"Can I go, *bhaiya?*" the man's voice snapped Jeevan back into the present.

Jeevan dismissed him politely, feeling slightly guilty for making the poor man wait. He stared as the man walked out of the supervisor's cabin, the glass door closing behind him. It had been two weeks since Raghuvir had named Jeevan as his assistant following which he had stopped coming to the yard completely, forcing almost all his duties on Jeevan. This change had come as a beacon in the darkness for him as it meant more money and a bigger opportunity to help the workers.

He had dedicated countless hours of work after his little promotion, making a few tweaks here and there. He had fixed all the water supply lines and had opened all the locked bathrooms. He still didn't consider it enough because, though fixed, the number of workers in the yard were too many for everyone to use the limited number of facilities in a civilised manner. There had been times when Jeevan had had to step in and break physical fights between workers over an issue like who would use the toilet first.

Jeevan looked up at the ceiling and sighed. The last few months felt like a few years to him as he sat and thought about the events that had unfolded over time. It had been more than a year since his arrival but he couldn't recall a second incident affecting him as much as the one with Aman did. Although intense at the beginning, the terrible anxiety about the money lost slowly faded over time as he earned more. The emotional damage is what he could not get over no matter how much he tried. He stood up and walked out of the cabin. The weather was pleasant but the environment in the yard was similar to what it was every single day, noisy and smoky.

Jeevan walked down the yard looking around to see if there was anything he could help anyone with. Ever since he had become the supervisor's assistant, he had been pretty overworked every day but he never turned down anyone who approached him seeking help and the workers loved him for this. He was like the supervisor they had never had.

In a year, Jeevan had already done more for them than Raghuvir had done since his joining as the supervisor. Many had even approached and supported him with the idea of applying for the post of supervisor. Jeevan suddenly noticed something out of the corner of his eye. He turned around to see one of the workers defecating out in the open by the shore. Jeevan felt a certain irritation in his bones as he picked up his pace and walked towards the man.

"How many times have I told them to use the washroom? Why don't they understand?" Jeevan mumbled to himself as he walked towards the man.

The man was coming back to the yard when Jeevan reached him. "Ramu *chacha*, how many times do I have to ask you to use the bathroom in the yard?" Jeevan's tone was a little harsher than he would have liked.

The poor old man clearly got intimidated as he folded his hands and replied, "I know *baba,* but what can I do? It is always occupied by someone or the other."

Jeevan sighed. He was expecting this answer as this has been a common problem for a while, amongst many other problems. He apologised to the old man for being rude and excused himself, continuing down the path towards the shore. Jeevan wanted to be left alone for a while, away from all these thoughts. It took him a few minutes to get to the shore.

It was not a proper beach, rather years of pollution had rendered it a useless one. There were metal scrap parts everywhere and the water had changed its colour slightly due to the constant drainage from the sewer pipe which was located close to the yard. Jeevan turned to look at the pipe as it made a loud gushing sound, depositing an enormous quantity of wastewater into the sea.

Jeevan felt an irritation in his throat as he started coughing once again, the bout lasting for a few seconds, leaving him in tears. He had been meaning to go see a doctor as suggested by quite a few people but hadn't gotten the chance to do so since he was overworked. As Jeevan stood wiping his tears a few feet away from the shoreline, a wave, one considerably bigger than normal, washed over his feet bringing something along with it. It collided with his left foot.

Jeevan panicked and stood completely still for a while as he had heard of jellyfish and sting rays being common in these parts. The water soon retracted all the way allowing him to look down at his feet. It was a fish, seemingly dead. Jeevan coughed a few more times, his throat still itchy as he bent down to touch the fish. He had heard of dead fish washing up on the shore due to the pollution but he had never witnessed it himself. The sightings had been getting more frequent over time.

Jeevan suddenly felt a hand on his shoulder as he turned around to see Darpana standing behind him, bent over and peeking over his back to see what he was looking at. Very few people knew about the incident between Jeevan and Aman, and Darpana was one of them. She knew Jeevan was in an extremely vulnerable state and needed all the support he could get. The responsibilities he shouldered for the workers on top of all this emotional turmoil just added to the burden. But she had developed respect and admiration for the man Jeevan had become.

"Another one. This is what, the sixth one in two days. Someone needs to stop dumping all this waste into the water," said Jeevan, looking at the dead fish.

Darpana grinned and asked, "That someone is you? How much more are you going to do?"

Jeevan sighed and replied with a hint of sorrow in his tone, "I haven't done enough. There are still so many things to work on. Most of them do not have a proper place to stay. They don't have the means to send their children to study which ultimately ends up with them being forced to work. They don't even get accident benefits, something that is their right. I don't know how to solve all these problems."

"You have come a long way, Jeevan. You will succeed in going through the rest of it as well. I will accompany you throughout…" Darpana was interrupted mid-sentence as they heard someone call out to them from behind.

The duo turned around in unison to see the office room security approaching them. He was quite old but was coming towards them quickly. He was trying to say something but his voice was drowned out by the crashing waves of the sea. It took him a few more seconds to cover the distance following which he bent down, trying to catch his breath and speak at the same time.

"Jeevan *babu*, it's a call for you from your home. It's urgent."

CHAPTER 20

HOME

The forest was filled with the chirping of birds accompanied by the croaking of frogs from time to time. The path was muddy and slippery, evident from the harsh rain that had affected the area. There was distinctive sloshing noise as the battery-powered rickshaw slowly crept down the wet road.

"The last three days have been a disaster, *babu*. We haven't seen rainfall this harsh for the last few years," said the auto driver to a distracted Jeevan sitting in the passenger seat.

Jeevan stared out at the road, all too familiar, as emotional nostalgia took hold. It had been three days since the fateful phone call that day, following which Jeevan had returned to West Bengal. It was his mother. She had fallen very ill and the medicines couldn't help her anymore. The news had hit an already shaken Jeevan like a train, leaving him completely lost. He boarded the first train he could get and started his journey home as soon as he possibly could, in the hopes of getting to see her alive for one last time.

Jeevan's thoughts took him back to the day when he received the call. It was his brother on the other side, calling to let him know about the news.

"Let me go with you, Jeevan," requested Darpana, after listening to the entire conversation.

Jeevan refused and said, "It's not the right time now. I need you to stay here and take care of things on my behalf. I don't trust Raghuvir."

But he was missing her now. Now was the time when he needed her support as terrible anxiety slowly overtook him. He was still quite some distance away from his village.

"Please speed up, *dada,*" Jeevan said in a low but serious voice.

After a couple more hours, Jeevan finally noticed the forest start getting less dense as they approached the tree line, marking the end of the forest and the beginning of his village. He kept staring out of the window, hand instinctively clutching his pants tightly as he laid his eyes upon the place he had called home since childhood. The sky was painted blue with occasional grey clouds passing overhead on an otherwise sunny day. He could see the same banyan tree from his dreams at a distance, resting quietly atop the small hill, beyond the village.

He could see the line of huts, one beside the other along the vast plots of farming lands in the area, stretching as far as the eye could see. One thing that caught Jeevan's attention was the accumulation of water in the fields ripe with crops, rendering the entire harvest completely useless.

"Those people must have suffered enormous losses," Jeevan said to himself, thinking about the farmers the lands belonged to.

Jeevan knew all of them really well as they used to help his family out with their harvests from time to time. A droplet of water fell on his arm as it slowly started to drizzle again. The sky was still clear, showing no signs of an incoming downpour. The anxiety within him tightened its grip as his hut slowly came into view. Even from a distance, Jeevan could see a few people standing outside his home as the realisation almost instantly dawned on him.

"Three hundred, *babu,*" the driver said quietly as he stopped the vehicle in front of the hut, the situation clear as day to him.

Jeevan slowly got off, silent tears camouflaged by the drizzling rain slowly streaming down his face, as he paid the fare. The small gathering outside the hut turned around in unison as they heard the rickshaw pull up behind them.

"*Dada?*" Jeevan heard the all too familiar voice before Krishna emerged from within the crowd and ran up to him to embrace him.

It was almost six in the evening before they finished with the traditions and rituals necessary after death. The funeral pyre still burnt strong in front of Jeevan, who was sitting on the ground, a few feet away from it. His brother was sitting beside him, a similar expression on his face, both of them stuck in a seemingly endless void within their heads. Jeevan had unbearable guilt building up inside him. His brother had told him everything about what happened over the last few days.

It started a few days ago. Due to the incessant rain, their mother had caught a very bad cold. Her asthma made things progressively worse as her lungs started to give out. The local doctors had given up hope and had suggested taking her to a big hospital in the city for treatment, but there was absolutely no means of transport available in the harsh rain.

It had been quite some time since he had got the first letter from Krishna following which he had decided to visit home soon. The guilt of not being able to keep that promise was overwhelming. He couldn't spend the last few moments with her, the woman who dedicated her entire life trying to give her children a decent, better one. To make things worse, he had stolen from them, or at least that is what his mind told him now.

"She died thinking of me as a thief," he mumbled inaudibly.

Jeevan's mumbling made Krishna snap out of his spiralling thoughts. He looked at Jeevan, concern written clearly on his face as he asked, "Are you okay, *dada?*"

"How can I be okay?" the reply was unexpectedly loud. Jeevan looked Krishna straight in the eyes and said, "I couldn't see her for one last time. We can't be with *maa* anymore, *bhai.*"

The rage subsided as quickly as it appeared as it was now replaced by an outburst of tears. Krishna held his brother as Jeevan buried his face in his chest and started howling like a baby. The fire from the pyre cast a huge shadow behind them on the ground and the drizzle continued ever so slightly. After a few hours, they finally got up and approached the funeral pyre.

The enormous fire wasn't there anymore. The only thing it left behind in its wake was a heap of grey ash. Jeevan brought out a clay pot which he placed on the ground beside the ash. The two brothers then took turns following their tradition where they picked up a fistful of ash from the heap, and touched it to their foreheads before they dropped it in the clay pot. It was almost midnight when they finally reached home.

Krishna approached a small plastic table which had two pots sitting on it and said, "She made this yesterday. She was very sick and I had asked her not to, but you know how she is, right? Never listens to us," Krishna smiled slightly as he lifted the cover of the utensils, revealing the cooked vegetables and curry.

Jeevan smiled as well before he realised something and the smile fell from his face. His brother noticed the change and asked him what the matter was.

"I do know what she '*was*' like, brother," Jeevan corrected him. There was a moment of silence between them before Jeevan took the food to the kitchen to heat it.

Krishna called out to him and said, "It might have gone bad *dada.*"

Jeevan turned around to face his brother and lifted the cover of the utensil. He placed his face near the pot, took a deep breath, and smiled as he said, "Can't wait to eat it."

Jeevan burped with satisfaction, making Krishna smile as they finished their meal. It had taken Jeevan less than five minutes to finish a plateful of rice, lentils and vegetables making it evident how much he missed his mother's cooking.

"I missed you, *dada,*" said Krishna sadly.

Jeevan placed his hand on his brother's shoulder, squeezing it lightly as he said, "I did too, *bhai.*"

CHAPTER 21

A NEW LIFE

The next few days passed in a blur as the two brothers spent their days receiving relatives and neighbours, and the nights fighting their grief and several other emotions, trying not to get overwhelmed. Jeevan had finally gathered the courage to ask Krishna about Bhoomi. He felt a pang of guilt as he was reminded of Darpana but he couldn't help asking about her. After all, the two had been close friends since a very tender age. Krishna told him how she had appeared at their front door that day with tears in her eyes. It was clear that she didn't want to marry a stranger.

She had cried her eyes out in front of their mother, telling her how she wanted to stay in the village and spend more time with them. Bhoomi had lost her own mother when she was born, the blame for which she had been forced to bear all this while. Her father disliked her and wanted to marry her to 'get rid of her' as he had quoted in the past. Jeevan's mother had been like her own, ever since they had met. She treated Bhoomi with utmost love and care. Hence, she would always be one of the first people she would approach with a problem.

Things had been especially hard on Jeevan as with each passing day, he felt worse and this information only added to the burden. It's not like he still had feelings for Bhoomi. Darpana was the only person he could truly think of whenever he tried to think of a potential partner. He had even gone to great lengths to imagine what their family would be like. Nevertheless, the guilt regarding Bhoomi was real and intense. He single-handedly blamed himself for ruining her entire life. But of course, all this was a secret he shared with no one.

He would look at the cot his mother used to sleep on and would constantly remind himself of how he couldn't be there for her when she needed him the most. Jeevan had tried doing everything. He tried taking walks around the village, to see the green forests, clear ponds and small hills but everywhere he visited, guilt followed him like a lap dog. He had visited most of these places with his mother for the first time, she had been the one to introduce him to them. They had comfort zones for him since his childhood. But not anymore, as every place he went to brought back old memories which fuelled the constant nightmares he'd been having since the day he arrived.

In the three days since his arrival, each night had been filled with restless thoughts, robbing him of sleep. The weariness had started to show on his face and Krishna had been quick to catch on. He realised that his older brother might try to escape all of this but had no idea about the things Jeevan was going through. Jeevan had even mentioned his wish to go back to Gujarat, sometime in the future when everything had settled down a bit.

This news had caught Krishna completely by surprise and he had started suggesting ways to keep Jeevan here ever since.

"What do you think about joining my school, *dada?*" asked Krishna.

It was past ten at night and the two brothers were sitting outside the hut, staring at the dark sky. Jeevan had missed this sky full of stars. A clear sky like this was impossible to see on any given day back in Gujarat, due to all the pollution. He was engrossed in his thoughts about Darpana and the ship breaking yard, and the pending responsibilities as an assistant supervisor were bothering him when Krishna's sudden question snapped him back to reality.

Jeevan hadn't told Krishna much about his work so his older brother had no idea of the man he had become. Krishna had always been the preferred child in the family and while that did not cause a problem among the brothers themselves, it made Krishna feel a weird sense of responsibility towards Jeevan, almost as if he was the younger brother. Jeevan was aware of this and admired his brother for it.

"You don't need to worry about me, *bhai*," Jeevan said in a reassuring tone, smiling as he turned to face his brother.

Krishna shook his head and replied, "No, don't think you can't. It's okay if you have forgotten how to write, I can teach you again. I will even teach you Hindi if you want. But don't go back to gas cutting."

Jeevan's smile was replaced by a frown as he realised how much his brother did not know about him. This was not the first time in the last few days that Krishna had offered to find work for him. He had previously offered more ideas instead of shipbreaking, which an already guilt-stricken Jeevan had forcibly considered doing.

"Wow, seriously?" asked Krishna, clearly impressed by what he was hearing.

Jeevan had taken the last thirty minutes to explain how much had happened over the last thirteen or fourteen months and that he was the assistant supervisor of the yard.

Krishna had a very childlike look on his face as he asked, "So can you speak English as well?"

Jeevan smiled as he said, "Not very good, but I can," slowly but perfectly.

Krishna let out a low whistle as a smiling Jeevan turned to look up at the sky once more, his thoughts quickly taking him back again.

"I have to go back, *bhai*. I have people waiting for me there, people who need my help," he said and then his smile grew wider as he continued, "I also have someone I want to call tomorrow. I have realised that life is too short to spend it away from your loved ones."

He got up and paused briefly to close his eyes, thinking of Darpana. "Too short to keep your feelings buried, afraid of what others might think," he finished saying before he walked back into the hut, leaving Krishna sitting with more questions than answers.

★★★

"It's all because of you," came his father's voice as he sat up in his bed, beads of sweat forming on his temple.

It was yet another nightmare, except this time it was almost dawn. Jeevan felt a heavy feeling in his chest as he started coughing. He got up to look for some water and noticed that Krishna's bed was empty. He drank a full glass of water, and a burning sensation built in his chest as another bout of vigorous coughing followed. After ten more painful minutes of panting and retching, the heaviness finally left his chest as he slumped down on his cot trying to catch his breath.

A few minutes later Krishna walked in through the door, a pot in his hand as he looked at Jeevan and said, "Did you go and start smoking there?"

Jeevan looked at his brother as if he was being ridiculous and shook his head in denial. Then he looked at the pot in Krishna's hand and asked in a raspy voice, "Still defecating out in the open?"

Krishna smiled and replied, "What to do brother? We don't have proper facilities like you people do in the big cities. So, we make do."

Jeevan knew Krishna was not being sarcastic. He was reminded of the workers once again as he said, "That couldn't be further from the truth, my brother."

The morning started early for Jeevan once again, as he could not go to sleep the previous night. Krishna was fast asleep when Jeevan left the house at sunrise and walked around the village. He went atop the small hill and sat under the banyan tree for a while, looking upon the beauty of the village as the rising sun slowly lit up the entire area. After a while, he made his way down to the village bazaar until the small yellow stall came into sight.

Even from this distance, Jeevan could read the sign very clearly, 'Chotu's phone booth.' The majority of the people living in the village did not own phones so they resorted to this telephone booth whenever they had to contact someone in another part of the city or country. Jeevan reached the booth, a piece of paper containing Darpana's number clutched in his closed fist. He approached the booth and dialled the number. It rang a few times before someone on the other side picked up the line.

"Hello?" said a familiar voice, bringing an instant smile to Jeevan's face.

"Hello Darpana, it's me, Jeevan," he replied.

The conversation then went on for the next fifteen minutes as Jeevan expressed his wish to return to her and start a new life. He also spent a great deal of time asking about the workers and what the work conditions were like.

"Everything is fine over here, Jeevan. I can't wait for you to return," Darpana said, her voice filled with longing.

Jeevan felt his face flush as he quickly said the next words and hung up before giving her a chance to reply, "I will be back soon, I promise. I love you, bye."

He slammed the receiver down, his chest pounding as childish excitement filled his head. For the first time in a while, he felt alive, a newfound hope in his chest.

But his moment of happiness was very short-lived as a voice from behind said, "Twenty rupees, *dada.*"

Jeevan turned around to see the stall owner, almost the same age as him, with a sheepish grin on his face since he had overheard the things Jeevan had said over the call. Embarrassment overtook Jeevan as he quickly paid the money and raced out of the market area.

There were shops of all kinds in the small market but it was nowhere nearly as populated as the markets in Gujarat usually were. There was a blue-coloured stall in the middle of the market which read 'Tickets available here.' The shop caught Jeevan's attention as he had never seen it before. He saw a middle-aged man sitting in the shop, in front of a computer.

Jeevan slowly made his way over to the shop and asked the person, "Are you new here?"

The man looked up from the computer for a brief second before replying, "Yes, we opened two days ago."

Jeevan was unsure of the decision he took next but he had a good feeling about it.

CHAPTER 22

TIME FLIES

Eleven Years Later

"He has completely changed, Satya. You don't understand," said Darpana, her voice breaking slightly.

She looked out of the window. A tree stood just outside it. The entire thing was devoid of any life except for a solitary leaf which hung from one of the higher branches. There was a huge pile of dead leaves, presumably from that tree itself, lying just below it. Darpana kept staring as a strong autumn breeze flew down the streets, scattering the pile all over the place and making the single leaf on the tree flutter vigorously as it held on to the branch for its dear life.

"I understand, *di*. But it's our Jeevan, I'm sure he'll pull through. He always has. Look at everything he has done in the last few years. The workers are all happy working in the yard, thanks to him. I know he has been acting a bit different recently, but he'll be okay," said Satya as he sipped the steaming hot cup of tea.

Satya had changed a lot in appearance. He had grown a moustache and was wearing a checkered shirt which did a poor job of concealing a big tummy which had formed over the years. The same couldn't be said for Darpana though. She still had her black flowing hair, which now extended down to her waist and her face had the same glow it did eleven years ago.

"I know he has pulled through in the past. But this time it is different. He isn't letting me through. He never does that and it worries me. I'm afraid he won't be able to hold on for much longer under all this pressure," replied Darpana as another strong breeze filled the room, making the windows rattle.

Darpana looked outside once more to see the leaf cling on for a few more seconds before it was finally carried away by the wind.

"After all, no one can continue holding on alone," she sighed as she closed the window.

It had been eleven years since Jeevan's mother's death. Following her demise, Jeevan had returned to Gujarat with newfound hope, a hope to forge something out of his then seemingly broken life and to stop dwelling on his past experiences. The first day at work after his return had been anxiety-riddled as he kept a lookout for Darpana. He had expressed his feelings for her over a phone call and had abruptly hung up after, giving her no chance to respond.

Though ecstatic at first, the feeling slowly converted into nervousness as he travelled across the country. His brother wasn't the happiest on hearing his decision but had been very understanding. Darpana welcomed Jeevan with open arms clearing all the doubts and anxiety bothering him. Their relationship blossomed over the years as they eventually moved in together.

Another surprise awaited Jeevan's return. One morning, shortly after his trip, a white envelope with a red stamp appeared on the supervisor's desk. It was Raghuvir's transfer order. It had finally come through and the entire yard was beside itself with joy. Raghuvir had been nothing short of a menace to them for several years and his transfer meant an end to their suffering. Their joy escalated even further as someone from within the crowd yelled out Jeevan's name. A few more people joined in and eventually, the entire yard started chanting his name.

The next series of events happened really fast, as after a strong recommendation thanks to a collective effort from the workers, Jeevan became the new supervisor. Jeevan hadn't taken a break since then. He started working more hours and putting in more effort now that he had more control over things. Due to his contribution, the yard saw major changes over the years. At present, there was not a single worker who could complain about pay rights, toilet or water facilities and the quality of equipment being used at the yard.

Jeevan, in fact, became a sort of inspiration across the city for other shipbreaking yards as the changes he brought benefitted workers throughout the industry. It hadn't been as easy as he had anticipated it to be, though. He met obstacles at every phase. Though smaller at first, as the problems grew in size, so did the hurdles. The most recent struggle had been almost two years long as Jeevan had attempted to address and create awareness about the living conditions of the workers. His goal was to get rightful occupancy for the workers in the living quarters that had been provided to them by the government.

He had found out that the quarters had been rented out to corrupt officials who in turn used the buildings to earn money by renting them out for various purposes, giving rise to a legal battle. The case was in Jeevan's favour and that of the workers. But unfortunately, time was not. The struggle went on for over two years with baseless allegations and a ridiculous amount of corruption, following which they got access to the living quarters which they now called home.

A number of people, both inside and outside the yard had considered Jeevan equivalent to a deity for all this. But along with the industry, certain changes could be seen in Jeevan's personality as well. He had expected hardships along the way but never had he imagined that it would eventually reach a point where he would become exactly like the other men who managed shipbreaking yards. He started spending more than twelve hours a day, six days a week at the yard, supervising the workers, lost amongst the sound of machinery as the days passed.

His relationship with Darpana was also strained as he felt it best to keep her out of everything for her own well-being. Darpana, on the other hand, being his constant companion for the past decade could not figure out what had happened to the man she had come to love so dearly. But unknown to her, there was another secret, a big one, that Jeevan had managed to keep hidden for quite some time now.

CHAPTER 23

IT'S GETTING WORSE

Jeevan stared at the light which had been built into the ceiling, admiring the intellect of the architect as the doctor asked him to cough once more. He felt the cold sensation of the stethoscope's metal tip once, the doctor pushing it hard against his chest as he listened silently. Jeevan was then asked to dress and sit while the doctor washed his hands and took a seat across the table. He pulled out the big white envelope that Jeevan had brought along with him and pulled out a dark film of an X-ray from within.

He took a few moments to study the film before he took a deep breath and said, "I don't need to say it, Jeevan *babu*. You know that it is getting worse. You need to stop working."

Jeevan had had this very conversation numerous times before, so he knew what was about to follow. As expected, the doctor wrote a new prescription for his medicines and once again asked him to take care of himself as his condition was getting worse. Jeevan politely received the prescription and made his way out of the clinic, half distracted the entire time. It had been almost four years since his diagnosis of chronic obstructive pulmonary disease or COPD as the doctor called it. Apparently, the constant exposure to the toxic smoke released by gas cutting had caused severe, almost irreversible inflammation and scarring in his airway. He had been experiencing coughing bouts for the longest time but it was when the breathlessness started, that the people around him got worried and forcibly sent him to the doctor.

They wanted to accompany him but he had insisted on making the appointment alone. Jeevan had refused to stop working despite repeated requests from the doctor, who kept trying his best to keep his patient's health intact through various medicines and inhalers. But all of these attempts just delayed the inevitable as the X-ray revealed that Jeevan's air passage had narrowed by almost seventy per cent due to the scarring.

Jeevan barely had any time to think about this though as his mind was fixated on the meeting that he was heading to. It was supposed to be very important and he needed to be in his best form for things to work out, so he couldn't afford to get distracted by the same thing he had been living with for the past forty months.

There had been an incident at the yard a couple of days ago where some of the debris from the broken ships had fallen on a yard worker called Maqsood, instantly snapping his leg into two. Jeevan had called for immediate medical care but to no avail as the medical facilities around them had no means to treat an open fracture. It took more than two hours for an ambulance to get there and one more before the poor guy finally reached a hospital and received proper care. Due to the delay and massive blood loss, there was a significant chance that Maqsood would lose his leg, making him a cripple and leaving him with no means to work and support his family. Jeevan was deeply shaken after this incident and decided to take up the issue with his superiors and get proper medical facilities for his fellow workers.

He walked for another twenty minutes before he reached the small one-storey building tucked away in the corner of the street. It was called the head office but the cabin was no bigger than his supervisor's office back in the yard. He walked in reluctantly to see a middle-aged woman sitting behind a small desk, busy watching something on her phone, totally unaware of the fact that she had company.

Jeevan cleared his throat, finally getting some response out of the woman as she looked up, clearly irritated as she asked, "*Kya chahiye?*"

Jeevan responded politely, "I'm here to meet the boss. I'm Jeevan."

The woman's eyes widened a bit as if she was expecting his arrival. She gestured towards a door at the back of the room as she said, "Sir is waiting for you."

He made his way over to the other end of the room and knocked on the door. A voice beckoned him from within after which he entered the room. It was a dirty and poorly furnished room with a slightly obese man of short stature sitting in the corner on a sofa, a glass of whiskey in front of him. Jeevan instantly felt hesitation kick in as he approached the man and took a seat.

The man was reading a magazine and did not bother to acknowledge his presence until Jeevan finally lost his patience and blurted out, "Sir, I'm Jeevan. The supervisor of the shipbreaking yard close to Ramnagar. I called you yesterday to..."

He was interrupted mid-sentence as the man got up, took the glass of whiskey in his hands and gulped it down in one go before he said, "I know, Mr. Jeevan. You have become quite the sensation amongst the workers in the past few years. They all love and respect you dearly. In fact, it was getting irritating, so I decided to meet you."

Jeevan clearly distinguished the hostility in his voice as he continued, "Listen. I know you have prepared a police report and want to take action against this but we don't have the funds for it. I have pressure from above and I can't let you file this complaint."

The man walked back to his desk in the centre of the room and opened the drawer to bring out a small envelope. Jeevan already knew what was coming next.

The man approached him, his face maintaining the same scowl as he held out the envelope towards him and said, "Take this like every other supervisor does and forget that we ever had this conversation."

Jeevan looked down for a few seconds, trying his best to maintain his composure as his insides screamed with anger.

After a while, he looked up and said with a smile, "Keep the money, Sir. We supposedly do not have the funds."

He got up and started to make his way out of the office when the man yelled out from behind, "Do as you please. But if that report reaches the police, you will lose your job."

Jeevan halted for a second, preparing to make a retort when his innate respect for professional conduct came to the fore and he walked out of the door.

CHAPTER 24

SECRETS

The sun had set by the time Jeevan reached his neighbourhood, a chill in the air marking the end of the autumn season. Jeevan took a deep drag of the *beedi* one more time before he dropped it on the ground and put it out with his shoe. This was another secret that Jeevan had kept from the world. It had been a few years since he had picked up this habit. He wasn't addicted to it but the tobacco helped release the pressure from his head. He liked cigarettes better but they were quite expensive to smoke daily so he had to make do with the *beedi,* which was the same as a cigarette except smaller and cheaper.

Jeevan always wondered why it was cheaper compared to cigarettes. The answer to this was given by a worker friend of his who had told him that it contains wood shavings along with tobacco, which is majorly injurious to health. Jeevan had paid no attention to his words as the idea seemed unbelievable to him.

After putting the *beedi* out, he thrust his hands in his pocket and started fishing for something until he finally pulled out a stick of chewing gum. He tore the wrapper and put it inside his mouth. Jeevan halted just as his house came into view and took a few more minutes to make sure there wasn't any kind of smell coming from his body.

All these years he had kept his habit hidden from Darpana and even his own doctor and he planned to keep it that way. After being satisfied, he made his way over to the front door of his living quarters and rang the bell. The quarters, though not luxurious, were definitely a major improvement from the slum they used to live in. Each of them had separate bedrooms, kitchen and bathroom with water facilities available at all times. The door opened with a slight creak followed by a slight cry from Jeevan as his friend walked out to embrace him. It had been almost six years since they had last seen each other since Satya had to leave the city for his family. They had had numerous conversations over the telephone but could not meet even once.

"What a pleasant surprise," said Jeevan, joy evident on his face.

Satya pulled back from the embrace and made a sniffing gesture as he eyed Jeevan from top to bottom.

"The same can't be said for you though, my friend. You've lost weight and have also started smoking," he said with a mischievous smile on his face.

Jeevan instantly stepped back a little, clearly embarrassed as he lowered his voice and said, "Keep your voice down. Darpana doesn't know."

Satya burst out laughing as he said, "That woman has the nature of a wild cat. I've come to realise that in the short time that I got to know her. Trust me, by now she knows."

Jeevan thought deeply again and Satya clearly saw him zone out. He frowned and said, "She's not here though. She went to a neighbour's house. Come inside."

Jeevan nodded and let out a clearly forced smile as he walked inside the house.

"How has your family been? And what brings you here again?" asked Jeevan as he took a seat on the old sofa.

Their quarter had two rooms and one dining space with a separate bathroom.

Satya took a seat beside him, frowning once again at the question, as he said, "Must you bring up the most serious topics now?"

Jeevan looked at him, a little surprised. Satya had left Gujarat all those years ago due to a family emergency. His wife in West Bengal had been pregnant with a boy and he had returned to welcome his son into this world. But a series of unfortunate events led to the demise of the infant after he was struck with illness shortly after birth. The incident had taken a huge toll on Satya and his family following which he chose to stay back with his wife and parents. Jeevan knew about the situation and hence had asked about his family's well-being out of genuine concern. Therefore, Satya's nonchalance surprised him a little.

"As for your other question, I got a job offer. I'm here to interview for it."

Jeevan was just about to respond when Satya asked him again, "What's up with you? When did you start smoking?"

His mischievous grin had returned followed closely by Jeevan's embarrassment. He laughed hard as he noticed the flush on Jeevan's face. But his laughter was cut short as he noticed the sudden seriousness in his friend's voice as he said, "Darpana can't know, Satya."

Satya smiled as he put one hand on Jeevan's shoulder and replied, "She won't, my friend."

Then suddenly, as if to change the topic Satya quickly picked up the documents Jeevan had placed on the table and started going through them. Jeevan sat up with a jolt, reaching out to snatch the documents out of his hands when he stopped abruptly. Satya looked at him, waiting for him to say something but with a gesture, Jeevan asked Satya to continue. Satya looked confused as he turned back to read the documents. Jeevan wanted him to know. He figured that since Satya was not a part of his life in Gujarat, sharing his secrets with him might actually help because he had already come to know about one. He sat observing his friend's expressions as Satya read the police report he had planned to file.

"This is good work that you're doing, Jeevan," he said, an impressed look on his face as he continued, "Darpana did say that you were doing some excellent work for the shipbreaking community but I didn't know to what extent. I know now."

Jeevan smiled a little, a hint of sorrow in his voice as he replied, "I do what I can, but it's not easy. I have no idea what I'm going to do with this report."

He then took the next fifteen minutes to tell him about the events that had unfolded in that office, earlier that day.

Satya let out a low whistle at the end of Jeevan's narrative and said, "Lose your job? That's huge. But I've got to tell you, my friend, you have changed a lot. I can barely see that timid and lost young boy. I see a confident man now."

He got up and walked towards the open window, got a packet of cigarettes out and lit one. He then turned around and held his arm out towards Jeevan, gesturing for him to take one.

Jeevan was very hesitant and started making excuses to which Satya replied with a smile, "She doesn't have to know who it was."

A few minutes later the two friends could be seen standing next to each other, sharing a solitary cigarette as a familiar nostalgia kicked in.

"She's a lot like you, you know?" Satya looked at him.

A car passed by on the street, making a loud honking noise as the two friends turned to look towards it in unison. They kept looking at it, anticipating that it would stop and for something to happen but it just kept going till it was out of sight.

"Darpana. A fitting name," he smiled once again as he put the cigarette out.

Jeevan turned to look out once more. It was not the first time someone had told him about the similarities that existed between him and Darpana. They had come a long way and it hadn't been easy at all, considering the societal pressure of a widowed woman living with a man younger than her. Satya walked back to the table, suddenly distracted by something.

Jeevan asked, "What's wrong, Satya?"

Satya took a few more moments to study the report lying in front of him, after which he told Jeevan, "I think I can help you out. I know this NGO, just outside Ramnagar. I knew the person who runs the NGO a long time ago. I think he might be able to help you with this."

Jeevan was confused by now. He asked, "But why? I can just go to the police. I'm not afraid of threats. They can fire me if they want to."

Satya looked at him and said, "I know you're not afraid but it's not about that. You won't be able to help the workers any further if they fire you. Also, why do you expect the police to care about a matter like this? They have so many other cases pending that you'll probably grow old by the time they start working on this case. And last but not the least, even if the police take some action against this case, your superiors can just bribe them and keep their mouths shut. You don't know how the world works my friend. Everyone is not so innocent."

He took a break to sip some water from the cup placed on the table. Jeevan looked concerned. The same half serious half dead look, signifying his deteriorating health dawned on his face as he leaned back and closed his eyes, mumbling something to himself all the while.

"This is why you should let your friends into your life. They help you walk in the right direction when you feel lost," said Satya smiling slightly.

Jeevan opened his eyes and looked at him, instantly realising what he was trying to get at as he asked, "What did she tell you?"

Satya sighed deeply and said, "Only that you've been completely absent for the longest time. The yard is your life now and your life is in the yard. You have become completely dedicated to your work and don't talk about home at all. What's wrong my friend? What is it that's bothering you? You can tell…" his voice drifted off mid-sentence as he noticed the hospital reports under the documents.

He looked at Jeevan, confusion written clearly on his face as he picked up the report and started going through it slowly. A part of Jeevan wanted to stop him as soon as possible but there was another part of him that wanted someone, at least, to know the truth.

It took Satya a few minutes to read the entire thing, following which he turned to look at Jeevan, a hint of worry in his voice as he asked, "You're going to be okay, right, *bhai?*"

Just as Jeevan was about to respond, the front door creaked loudly as Darpana walked in, a few plastic bags in her hand as she almost stumbled onto the ground. She placed the bags on the ground and closed the door behind her with a loud thud. Satya looked back at a wide-eyed Jeevan who was clearly distressed, as he frantically shook his head in an attempt to tell him to not let Darpana know. It took her two seconds to figure out that someone had been smoking in the room as she made a sniffing noise and turned to look at Satya.

"You need to slow down on the smoking, Satya. You'll fall sick like this. Tell him, Jeevan."

Jeevan looked at her and then at Satya and said very awkwardly, "Yes you should stop, my friend."

Satya burst out laughing as he replied, "Yes, I will smoke less. But before all that, Darpana, I want to show you something."

Jeevan looked horrified as he saw Satya pick up one of the documents from the pile before he gave it to Darpana and continued, "See what our Jeevan has been up to."

Jeevan instinctively grabbed Satya's arm tightly and looked him in the eye, anger welling up inside him.

Satya unexpectedly replied to his stare, "No brother. You have kept enough secrets. You need to let us help you."

Darpana stared at him for a while before she opened the document and started going through it. It was at that point when Jeevan finally noticed the paper in her hand. It wasn't his medical records. It was the police report that he had put together. Relief washed over him as he saw Satya looking at him, devoid of any expression.

It was late in the night, a few hours after dinner. The three of them sat in a circle, a heap of papers in the middle. Satya and Darpana had managed to convince Jeevan to not file the police report and risk losing his job. They instead decided to rely on the power of the common people and resolve this issue by creating awareness amongst the masses.

"I will talk to Daniel. I'm pretty sure he'll be able to help us to a great extent with this. He and his NGO have been doing some extremely good work for the common people and so they have great reach."

Jeevan seemed satisfied with this approach. For the first time in a while, he did not feel a deathly burden hanging over his head. It felt good, to share his problems with these people and look for a solution together. Something he had truly forgotten to do, all these years. Jeevan looked at Darpana, zoning out as Satya continued talking about Daniel, the head of the NGO. For a few moments, he forgot about everything going on in his life and stared at her. He remembered the countless beautiful moments he had shared with her over the years. Then, suddenly, for the first time in over six years, Jeevan was reminded of his home, his brother, whom he had not talked to for the longest time.

"What have I been doing with my life?" he was wonderstruck as he asked himself this question.

He suddenly felt an itch in his throat, a familiar feeling that acted as a reminder. He got up and excused himself as he walked towards the bathroom and locked himself in, a daily ritual by now. Jeevan then proceeded to bring out the tablets prescribed to him and gulped them down along with some water from the sink. There was a small mirror above the sink. He splashed some water on his face and looked at himself in the mirror, wondering how much longer he could keep up this charade.

CHAPTER 25

A VISIT TO THE HOSPITAL

The bustle of the city grew louder as Jeevan made his way through the busy streets. He had a plastic bag in his hand which contained a dozen bananas. He was on his way to the hospital where Maqsood, his fellow worker, had been admitted after the incident. It had been a few days since the incident and the doctors, unfortunately, had to amputate the lower portion of his leg. Since there had been too much blood loss, by the time they got to a hospital the choice was either that or death, making the decision comparatively easier. While relieved at first, Maqsood and his family were quickly struck with grief again as they realised that he wouldn't be able to work for the rest of his life.

Jeevan felt a pang of familiar guilt creep up his spine as he noticed Maqsood's family walking in through the entrance, just a few feet away from him. He didn't know whether he should go and talk to them. He did consider himself partly at fault for the incident after all. Maqsood's wife and his two children slowly walked up the crowded lobby of the government hospital, followed closely by Jeevan. The hospital was in a sorry state as there were patients all over the place due to the lack of rooms. Jeevan saw a woman kneeling beside an old man lying flat on a stretcher, crying her eyes out. He didn't know whether the man was dead or not. They climbed the stairs to enter the male general ward, where Maqsood had been admitted. This was the second time that Jeevan had come to visit him, the first time being with Darpana when he was still unconscious.

Maqsood's family went in and Jeevan patiently waited for them to have their time together while he spent that time looking at the other patients admitted to the ward. The first thing that caught Jeevan's attention was a young kid, in his early teens, sitting on one of the beds with a mobile phone in his hands, surrounded by a doctor and a nurse. At first glance, Jeevan could see nothing wrong with the boy. But as he kept staring curiosity got the better of him. There were several other beds in the big ward but not one of them had any other patient of his age and almost all of them had a visible illness or injury of some sort. Jeevan made his way into the room and stood close to the boy's bed so that he could hear their conversation. The doctor had drawn the curtains and stepped to the side along with the nurse. They were talking amongst themselves, unmindful of the eavesdropping.

"It's not looking good, sister," the doctor said with concern, "The cancer is growing much faster than we expected. It has spread to his liver now. It's time to inform the parents, there's nothing much we can do now."

He then handed the file he was carrying over to the nurse and left the room in a haste, leaving her staring at the boy with a certain sadness in her eyes.

"Cancer," thought Jeevan.

He had heard of the disease before. Several workers in the yard claimed to have lost family members to this disease. It was deadly and grew fast and apparently didn't have a specific cure. All you can do is fight it with different treatments and hope to survive. Jeevan was pulled out of his thoughts all of a sudden as he found the same nurse staring at him. He realised he had been staring at her all this while and quickly broke eye contact as he walked out of the room.

"Excuse me, sir," a voice came from behind as he turned around to see her walking towards him. "Are you here to see someone?" she asked as she stopped in front of him.

Jeevan stuttered a bit as he said, "Umm yes, I'm here to see Maqsood, I work with him."

The nurse eyed him from top to bottom before she nodded and asked Jeevan to follow her as she started walking in a different direction. She guided him to the end of the room where Maqsood lay on his bed, surrounded by his family. Jeevan felt the same guilt in his chest yet again as he laid his eyes on the poor man. He was covered in bandages, with wounds all over his hands and head due to the sharp metal from the debris. But the worst of all was his leg, which was cut in half, the end covered in a thick coating of gauze, which had slowly started to change colour from white to red.

"You have a visitor," the nurse broke the silence abruptly as the four of them turned to look at Jeevan in unison.

"Jeevan *bhaiya*?" Maqsood cried out just as the nurse finished talking.

Jeevan looked at the nurse who seemed content with the fact that they knew each other before walking away.

Jeevan went closer and handed the bag to Maqsood as he said, "These are for you, my friend. Eat them and become strong so we can get you out of here." Maqsood's face lit up with a smile, as did the rest of his family's.

It was around two in the afternoon when Jeevan left the hospital. It had been raining for the last few days but the sun was out today. The heat, in fact, was unbearable and the asphalt felt like a frying pan. Every step he took sent heat waves up from the pavement towards his feet as he made his way to the yard. It was not the hot weather that was bothering him, even though he was drenched from head to toe in sweat. The conversation with Maqsood was running on a loop in his head. The man had been working there for many years and was a dedicated employee, but now he was just a liability. Or so he considered himself.

He was worried that he wouldn't have a job as the industry was labour intensive and there wasn't any other work that he was good at. Jeevan was hoping that he could do something to help the man but wasn't sure how until Maqsood started talking about his family. When he did that, it made Jeevan think about his own and the many responsibilities he had towards Darpana. He thought about the dreams he had for the two of them. He thought about how she had sacrificed so much for him and his dedication towards his work.

He thought about his dead parents after Maqsood spoke about his own and all that they had tried to give him. Most of all he thought about the future he had planned for himself and Darpana, none of which could be achieved without money. Money that Maqsood needed desperately. The non-stop chain of thinking came to a halt as the entrance to the shipbreaking yard slowly came into sight. Jeevan sighed and smiled a bit as he approached the front office and signed his name. He smiled at the receptionist who gave him a concerned look before she turned to look back towards the office.

"He's here again, sir," the woman told him after a few moments of silence.

"Again?" Jeevan's eyes widened, glowing bright with anger.

He stormed towards his office, fists clenched as he tried his best to maintain his composure. He could already see the old man standing outside his office, staring at the shoreline. He had come across the man a few weeks ago outside the yard. He had felt pity for the man and had tried to offer him money but was turned away rather harshly. It became a daily routine for the man to cross Jeevan's path every morning from that day onwards. He had tried entertaining the man a couple of times by asking what he wanted but was met with the same reply every time.

The man said one thing and one thing only, "Go back home. You don't belong here. They have a different plan for you."

The line had almost been forged into Jeevan's mind due to the daily reminder. This was two or three days ago, just after the accident. Jeevan was going to the yard when he came across the man, sitting outside the entrance once again. But he was in no mood to entertain all that madness today. He ignored the man at first when he started chanting the same line again and walked through the entrance. Jeevan thought that would be the end of it but he couldn't be further from the truth.

As he signed his name in the register, the man walked up behind him and grabbed him by the hand, repeating the same line, only in a significantly louder voice. It didn't take long for the security to arrive and take him out of there after that. He had not been seen since. Jeevan had expected him to not show up again but he had clearly underestimated the 'madman' as they called him.

He walked up to the man and did not wait for even a second before he grabbed him by the arm and started dragging him away from the office, towards the gate. It took a few seconds for the old man to realise what was happening, after which he started shouting and throwing his hands about in an attempt to get out of Jeevan's iron grip. But he wouldn't let go.

"I've had enough of you. I've tried to help you, give you money, give you food. You won't take anything and instead of being grateful you come here and disrupt my workspace," he paused as he felt the itch in his throat and a heaviness in his chest. But as the man kept yelling Jeevan's anger got the better of him once more as he continued, "I'm taking you to the police. They will do what they see fit with you."

Nothing seemed to bother the old man as he was in a world of his own, screaming and laughing. But as the two of them got closer to the entrance, Jeevan felt the world around him start spinning. His heartbeat grew faster as he heard a high-pitched ringing inside his ears before a vigorous coughing bout kicked in. That was the only detail Jeevan remembered before everything went black.

CHAPTER 26

GREEN WAVY LINES

The heartbeat monitor beeped in a constant monotonous rhythm. Wires protruded from behind it and travelled all the way to the bed beside it and disappeared under the sheets. The monitor displayed green wavy lines, showing the beating rhythm of Jeevan's heart. Showing everyone that he was still alive. A visibly concerned Darpana and Satya stood on either side of the bed, staring at him as he lay unconscious on the bed. The door behind them made a creaking noise as two doctors walked in. One of them was Jeevan's original consultant.

They took several minutes to do certain examinations following which one of them left the room. Satya and Darpana stared at Jeevan's doctor from a distance, hopeful that he would proclaim him to be okay now.

Finally, when the doctor seemed to have completed his examination, Darpana walked up to him and asked, "He will be okay, right?"

The doctor turned towards her, a worried look in his eyes as he let out a huge sigh.

"How many times have I asked him to stop putting so much pressure on himself? He's supposed to stop working. His airway is getting narrower with each passing day. His heart will give out like this."

He noticed Darpana's eyes widen and her expression change to a horrified one as he spoke. He instantly realised that she had no prior knowledge about Jeevan's condition.

"Are you related to him?" the doctor asked.

But Darpana couldn't reply. She felt her world shatter around her as she slowly realised what the doctor was hinting at. Jeevan had kept his health condition a secret from her all this while. He had told her that everything was okay and he just needed to take a rest for a while before he got all better. All of that had been a lie. Satya understood the emotional turmoil Darpana was going through so he took the liberty of replying to the doctor himself.

"They live together, sir," he said, in an attempt to avoid any further conversation.

The doctor nodded and said, "Please take care of him and please keep him away from the yard," before walking out of the room.

The moment the door closed behind him, Darpana collapsed on the chair beside Jeevan and broke down completely. She covered her face in the bed sheets as she clutched his hands tightly. Satya could do nothing but watch, a memory of him sharing a smoke with Jeevan floating before his eyes as guilt gripped his heart tightly.

Three days passed in a blur. The first two saw Jeevan recovering in the hospital and on the third day he returned home. He was still in very poor condition and the doctor had strictly advised him to stay in bed for at least a month. He couldn't argue or rather was in no state to argue. His arms and legs felt like they would fall off the moment he got out of bed, such was his fatigue. Shortness of breath along with a low-grade fever had also been his constant companions ever since he regained consciousness. Jeevan didn't remember much from that day but one particular thing had stuck in his head.

"God has a different plan for you my child," the 'madman' had said these words before everything had gone black.

In these three days, Jeevan had told himself numerous times that he was mistaken. But he knew that the memory was too clear for it to have been a mistake. He just didn't know what to make of the situation. A knock on the door brought Jeevan back to reality as Darpana walked in quietly, followed closely by Satya. Jeevan looked at Darpana as she went and sat in a corner. She had been pretty quiet for the last few days, speaking to him only when necessary.

Jeevan figured that she was worried about him and was hence behaving unnaturally. Neither Darpana nor Satya had let him know the truth. It was Satya's idea to let him recover completely before talking to him about it.

He saw Satya smile as he asked, "How are you, *bhai?*"

Jeevan smiled and replied in a raspy voice, "Better now that you two are here."

He turned his head towards Darpana and smiled but failed to get a response out of her.

Satya sensed the tension in the air as he quickly interrupted and said, "I have news that will make you feel even better."

Jeevan's face lit up with curiosity as he struggled to sit up straighter in his bed. He had regained consciousness but his body felt like that of a dead man. His chest hurt with every little movement he made and his throat burned from having the breathing tube removed recently. A short coughing bout overtook him again as Darpana rushed to help him sit up and drink a glass of water. It took Jeevan a few minutes to regain his composure.

He looked at Satya once more and asked, "You were saying?"

The concerned look on Satya's face was wiped away as he pulled out his phone and fiddled with it for a while before handing it to him. Jeevan took the phone and looked at it, taking a few minutes to absorb all the information on the screen. Satya had walked up to his bed this time, a child-like expression on his face as he leaned in to join his friend.

"I don't understand. What is he trying to say?" Jeevan asked finally, losing patience.

Satya took the phone from him and started explaining, "This email is from my friend Daniel. I gave your report to him and told him about everything that you have done for these workers. I told him you needed help to further your cause and he was more than ready to help. Social media has gone viral over this news over the last two days. Their NGO managed to get through to the common people and now there are thousands of people all over the country signing petitions in favour of the shipbreaking yard workers."

Satya was panting by the time he paused, such was his excitement. He quickly took a sip of water from a bottle lying nearby before he continued speaking at the same pace, "You know what this means, my friend? People are demanding rights for the workers and they won't stop until they get what they want. Also, the cherry on top is that your superiors can't buy the population no matter how much money they have to offer. In any case, I hear they're running low on funds," Satya winked at Jeevan as he finished speaking.

Jeevan smiled and was about to say something in reply when a loud knock from the front door interrupted them. Darpana stood up without saying anything and went to receive whoever was at the door. Jeevan looked at Satya questioningly. The latter asked him to give her some time. They suddenly heard quite a few voices from outside. Satya looked at him and went to see what the commotion was about. Jeevan lay in bed, waiting. After a few minutes both Satya and Darpana walked in together, smiling, followed by about ten or twelve people who started entering the small room one by one till it was completely filled.

Jeevan felt his eyes tear up as he recognised every single face in the room. These were all workers from the shipbreaking yard, the people he worked with every day, the people he was struggling to do so much for. The realisation that the same people acknowledged and reciprocated his feelings was overwhelming at that moment for him. The next couple of hours were all about Jeevan talking his heart out for the first time in a while, in the presence of all these people. There was one thing that all of them insisted on though—that he needed rest. They asked him to take two or three months of medical leave and relax.

"We'll be waiting for you when you come back healthy and strong, Jeevan *bhaiya*," one of them said.

By the time they left, it was dark outside and Jeevan was filled with various emotions. He knew that he wasn't supposed to, but he wanted to go back to work more than ever, now that things were looking up for the workers and the industry. He had let the workers know about the public movement on social media and the support they were getting from all over the country. He swore to himself that he could see their faces light up and their chests puff out when they heard that the common people were supporting them and caring for their well-being.

Jeevan understood the feeling as he had been prey to that inferiority complex for the longest time. Whatever life he had spent outside his village, he was made to feel like he was inferior to most people out there. It was natural for these people to have faced the same kind of shaming, so public support guaranteed a boost in mental and emotional strength. Jeevan closed his eyes and made some calculations as to how many days of rest he would need before joining work again.

A few moments later, he had a satisfied look on his face as he whispered under his breath, "A week should be enough."

Almost instantly, as if in retaliation to his poor decision, his abdomen cramped up, followed by a stinging pain in the left part of his chest as he fell back on the bed. The shortness of breath made him start panting once more. Jeevan shut his eyes tightly as he waited for the pain to pass, which it did gradually.

A few moments later, he opened his eyes as he once again whispered, "Might need a bit more rest than that."

CHAPTER 27

FEELINGS
UNCONVEYED

The days got annoyingly similar as Jeevan had to helplessly follow the same routine every day. He used to get up in the morning, walk around the house as a sort of exercise, and do whatever chores he could as Darpana would be away at work. Almost two weeks passed like this. He felt slightly better with each passing day. And with that, the urge to rejoin work grew stronger.

Darpana understood the mental turmoil he was in while sitting at home, so she would try to bring some parts of the work back home and get Jeevan's opinion. And though this act of consideration helped him more than he would care to admit, it also made him miss work more. The petition-signing campaign across the internet had been a huge success, forcing Jeevan's superiors to cave in and pass the order for the development of medical facilities near the yard.

Moreover, someone, somewhere on the internet had brought another problem to light, something which Jeevan himself hadn't considered before. It was the lack of insurance for these people who were working under hazardous conditions. It didn't take long before this issue took the internet by storm as well. Satya had recently informed him that there was another petition going around the internet demanding strict life insurance policies for the workers and their families so that they have something to lean on after facing accidents as Maqsood had.

Lastly, Satya had taken the initiative to start a crowdfunding programme for Maqsood. The results were eye-opening as they managed to gather around ninety thousand rupees in just under two days, all of which they passed on to Maqsood and his family. The work environment was different now, according to Darpana.

Following these events, there had been a significant morale boost amongst the population of the yard. Things had finally started to look up for them and Jeevan himself couldn't be a part of it. There was only one thing holding him back, his physical condition. He had tried to do something a little labour intensive on numerous occasions, but even the slightest chores tired him out in an instant. Jeevan also felt a growing heaviness in his chest but didn't inform anyone about it since he was scared that he will be asked to rest longer.

One night, he felt different. For a change, there was no heaviness and his stamina seemed to have increased. For the first time in two weeks, Jeevan managed to stand in the kitchen for forty-five minutes straight as he prepared a meal of rice, lentils and potato curry. He was visibly happy that day, a sight that had gotten rare over the past few days. He finished cooking, washed the dishes and placed the food in separate utensils, and neatly arranged them on the table. It took him a few moments to take the next decision. He approached the front door of the house and put his slippers on, twisting the handle of the door. A cool breeze of air rushed in to greet him as he opened the door.

He walked down the road in silence, a certain chill in the air bringing about a dead feeling in the neighbourhood. It wasn't unusual at this time of the day as most of them were out working in the yard. Jeevan continued down the street until his eyes fell upon someone walking towards him from the opposite direction. It didn't take long before the familiar face came into view and as the two pairs of eyes met, they exchanged a thousand feelings. It was Darpana, coming back home from work, eyes wide open as if she couldn't believe what she was seeing.

Jeevan walked up to her and held her in a tight embrace as he told her, "See, I'm all better now."

It took her a few seconds to comprehend the situation after which she returned the embrace, the two holding each other in the middle of the street for a while. Then Jeevan pulled out of the hug as he took her hand in his own and started retracing his steps back home. It took Jeevan around ten minutes to meet Darpana, and they spent double the time walking home as they maintained a slow pace. Neither of them minded though. Their attention was completely on each other as they pointed out the little things they noticed around them. They picked up leaves and flowers from the road, feeling like young children again. They had missed this feeling in their relationship for the last few years and it proved to probably be one of the most beautiful moments in Jeevan's life.

But as every good thing has to come to an end, Jeevan found himself feeling the same as they walked up to the entrance of their house. Darpana brought the key out and was just about to open the door when he said loudly, "I want to go to the yard tomorrow. I won't work, I promise. I just want to be there once."

Darpana stopped just as she was about to open the door. She turned around to face Jeevan, all the past revelations which had been momentarily forgotten flooding her thoughts. As her expression changed, the same emptiness appeared in her eyes again.

Jeevan noticed it almost instantly as he finally decided to ask, "What's the matter, Darpana? You have been like this for the past few weeks. Is there something bothering you? Please tell me."

Darpana contemplated for a while and actually considered for a moment to let him know about everything that had been bothering her—the secrets that he had kept hidden for so long. But there was a small part inside her that screamed for her to not do it today.

"Today, of all days," she thought as she walked in through the door.

Jeevan had been feeling better after a long time and she didn't want to halt his progress by bringing this up now. She turned around as he closed the door and said, "Okay you can go to the yard tomorrow, but only for an hour."

She couldn't help but smile as she saw a childlike grin appear on his face after she finished. The rest of the night seemed like an eternity as Jeevan lay waiting for the sun to rise. The clock struck eight and Darpana had just gotten out of bed when she saw Jeevan already smartly dressed for work, looking out of the window. He was ready to go. She smiled as he waved at her and left in a hurry, joining the other workers passing by his house, all on their way to work. The walk from their quarters to the yard didn't take too long but it seemed like another eternity before they finally reached the gate. Jeevan looked ecstatic as he walked in, and was greeted by almost every person he came across.

"Jeevan *bhaiya*," he heard a cry come from behind as he turned around to see a few more familiar faces rush up to him. After a few moments of catching up one of them said, "Come see the *Sultana*."

Jeevan's eyes turned towards the mass in the distance. He had heard a lot about it but had never gotten a chance to see it since the ship had arrived after Jeevan got admitted to the hospital. It was probably one of the biggest ships to ever arrive at the yard. Jeevan slowly made his way over to the ship, staring up at the towering mass from below as a memory from the first day of his arrival at the yard came to mind.

He smiled as he said, "Let's go up there."

It took him ten minutes to climb to the top of the ship, followed by two of his colleagues as they walked along the railing of the deck. Jeevan had to climb quite a few flights of stairs, making the shortness of breath return and greet him once more, as he maintained a slower pace than the others, walking quite some distance behind them. He took a brief moment to halt and stare at the vast expanse of the ocean that lay behind them, the *Sultana* overlooking them all.

Suddenly, a high-pitched ringing replaced the sound of the strong breeze blowing at that height as a familiar pain took over, this time causing a stiffness over the left part of his body. He tried to open his mouth to call out for help but the force of the wind drowned out his now increasingly slurring speech. Jeevan felt the world start to spin as he felt himself start losing balance.

He shot his left arm out, in an attempt to grab the railing but the simultaneously increasing stiffness made him miss his mark as he completely lost balance and toppled over the railing. Time seemed to halt around him for a while as the ringing stopped and was replaced by a deathly silence, the only audible sound being a momentarily loud and distinct thud before everything went black.

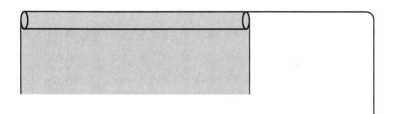

EPILOGUE

The rain lashed the ground, giving rise to a shroud of mist that encompassed the air around the yard. Several workers stood in front of the office, and all of them seemed lost in their thoughts. Satya stood at the head of the crowd, a red file in his hand and a grim look on his face. His voice was drowned out by the noise of the rain. The file carried good news but there was no joy on anyone's face. It had been more than a week since Jeevan's demise but it still felt like the incident had happened just a few hours ago. The days following the event proved disastrous for both the workers and their families.

"That completes the list of names. And don't forget to bring the insurance forms tomorrow," said Satya loudly, trying to make himself heard till the back of the crowd.

He then brought an umbrella out, opened it, and stepped into the rain as he held it over his head. Almost instantly, a wave of emotion overtook Satya as he found himself being dragged back to his memories… memories of his dear friend.

"You were supposed to be here, giving this news to them," he muttered to himself, lighting a cigarette as he walked down the wet road.

The industry had recently passed a new rule where all the workers, irrespective of gender, would get life insurance benefits for themselves and their families. This was a huge development for the yard and its workers, but the absence of the man who had made all of this possible caused an unbearable sadness. Jeevan had left an impact that the industry would remember for years to come and the workers could never thank him enough for it, not anymore at least.

There were numerous things Satya blamed himself for—the first and foremost being the inability to speak truthfully to his friend. He had advised Darpana to refrain from speaking to Jeevan about his health and smoking habits till he was doing better. He was thinking of the mental toll it would take on him. He hadn't thought about the physical toll it was already taking on him. A part of him knew that Jeevan couldn't have been saved no matter what, such was his condition. But he couldn't bring himself around to believe it. He suddenly felt a pang in his gut, a weird feeling that something was wrong. While wondering what the feeling was about, he recalled something. He took his phone out and dialled a number, placing the phone near his ear as he continued to smoke the cigarette. After a few rings, someone picked up the call.

"Darpana *di*, how are you? I was just at the yard and thought that I'd check up on you once," said Satya, trying his best to maintain a cheerful tone.

Darpana had been an emotional wreck after the incident. She had locked herself up in her house for the next three days, refusing to eat or drink anything. It did not take very long for people to start talking about Jeevan's death, which further worsened the situation. Satya had heard all kinds of comments passed by the people in the vicinity. Some called her cursed and said that she could never keep a man happy, others said that widowhood suited her best.

Satya thought it better to keep her away from the resulting trauma since Darpana didn't know about any of these vicious comments yet. Little did he know that certain people lacked any sort of humanity. There were a few men and women who despised her and held her responsible for Jeevan's death. They went to great lengths to call her a witch to her face. All of this added to the burden she was already carrying.

She shared Satya's guilt of not being able to have a heartfelt conversation with the man she had come to love so dearly. She held herself responsible for not being a more integral part of his life and for not taking care of him when he needed her. Satya had tried his level best to assure her otherwise, but she wouldn't listen. The comments from the people around her just increased the doubts she had in her mind.

After three long days of trying to hide from other people, Darpana finally mustered the courage to step out of the house to restock groceries. The moment she stepped out on the road, she felt everyone's gazes lock on her, one after another. She could see people whispering amongst themselves while a few stared at her with a certain hatred in their eyes. She felt a wave of emotion overcome her as she walked away from the place. She had not mentioned this to Satya though. She spent her days and nights crying, ending up with a scratchy voice.

But she tried to maintain her composure as she replied to his call, "Yes, Satya. I'm okay, what about you?"

As he listened to her voice, Satya felt a wave of relief wash away the previous discomfort spreading over his body. He sighed audibly. He then went on to tell her about the events of the day, hoping to keep her busy for a while so that she would have something else to think about. He kept talking as Darpana sat on the other side, holding the phone in her hand while staring silently at the empty bottle of rat poison lying in front of her.

Made in the USA
Columbia, SC
09 December 2022

73240180R00136